Hennessy

A NOTE ON THE AUTHOR

Vincent Banville was born in Wexford and worked
as a teacher, first in Nigeria and then in Dublin.
He is chief fiction reviewer of the *Sunday Press* and
author of a novel, *An End to Flight,* that deals with
the Biafran war. *Hennessy* is first of a series for
young people that also includes *Hennessy Goes
West.*

PRAISE FOR *HENNESSY*

"A raw, irreverent and, above all, genuinely comic
account of the rough-and-tumble adolescence of a
very contemporary Dublin schoolboy."

CHILDREN'S LITERATURE ASSOCIATION OF IRELAND GUIDE

"A colourful and hilarious account."

EVENING HERALD

Vincent Banville

Hennessy

POOLBEG

First published 1991 by
Poolbeg Press Ltd
Knocksedan House,
Swords, Co Dublin, Ireland
Reprinted 1992

© Vincent Banville, 1991

The moral right of the author has been asserted.

Poolbeg Press receives assistance from
The Arts Council / An Chomhairle Ealaíon, Ireland.

ISBN 1 85371 207 8

Cover design by Judith O'Dwyer
Set by Richard Parfrey in Stone Serif 10/14
Printed by Cox & Wyman Ltd Reading Berks

For my mother-in-law Mrs Bridgit McCabe

I would like to thank Colm and Douglas Banville, and the students of St Joseph's C.B.S. in Fairview, for helping me to get a peek into the teenage mind.

1

"You brat!"

Wielding her huge, knitted handbag like a hammer thrower, Mrs Margaret—call me Molly—Caskey made a swipe at her grandson, Michael Hennessy. Luckily for him she missed, but a plaster statue of St Anthony wasn't quite so lucky and took a nose dive to the floor.

Behind his desk Fr Mogue tut-tutted. His large, bloodhound's face registered disapproval but whether it was because of her missing her grandson or knocking the saint over wasn't clear. He put his hands together steeple fashion in front of his face and possibly said a silent prayer.

Hennessy, small and quick on his feet, was used to dodging. Although invariably presenting an innocent face to the world, trouble followed him about like his shadow on sunny days. He was the kind of person about whom Shakespeare said: "When troubles come, they come not single spies but in battalions."

And now he was really in it. Just before his grandmother had arrived like an avenging angel, the priest had delivered his sentence: "Exhausted our patiences... Ignored all warnings...Final chance..." —and then the dreaded word, to *him* if not to Hennessy —"Expelled!"

The truth was, if the poor man had only known it, that the apparently cowed boy standing in front of him had been trying to achieve such an objective for the best part of six months. Ever since his father had sent him home from Africa and enrolled him as a boarder in Assisi High School, he had been waging a battle to get himself thrown out. He had gone absent without leave, smoked in the dormitory, vomited in the swimming pool, and now, having managed to smuggle a large amount of quick-acting laxative into the morning porridge, he had gummed up the locks on the communal lavatories with UHU glue, leaving the majority of the occupants of the school in a state of grave emergency.

Retribution had been swift and final. To save him from the vengeance of the suffering pupils, the Principal, Fr Mogue, had locked him in his office. He had then sent for his grandmother to come and take him away. This time there would be no reprieve: "Think yourself lucky, boy," Fr Mogue had told him, "that you're not available to the tender mercies of those you have caused to suffer so abominably. They'd hang, draw and quarter you..."

His grandmother had pleaded on his behalf, although plainly seeing it as a lost cause, pointing out to the priest that Hennessy's parents were thousands of miles away in Africa: "Think of how they'll feel when they hear that their beloved son has been expelled...And from the very school that his own father attended. He was a model pupil, a sportsman and a scholar. It'll break his heart..."

But her pleas fell on deaf ears. Fr Mogue was adamant that Hennessy must go: "He'd be assassinated if he stayed now," the priest told Molly. "My dear woman, do you realise what he did? I can't guarantee his safety. I don't even know if I'd want to…"

It was then that Molly had made the swipe at Hennessy with her handbag that brought St Anthony low. Now both she and the priest stared at him and, to ward off their scrutiny, all he could think to do was to pick up the fallen saint and cradle him in his arms.

The priest cleared his throat, put his hands flat on the desk and stood up. It was obviously a movement of dismissal. "His belongings are here," he said, indicating Hennessy's duffel bag. "I think it would be expedient if you both went out by way of the window. A quick retreat would be the best course. He who turns and runs away etc. Any further details can be attended to by letter…"

He opened the French window, looked out cautiously, then stood aside. "The coast is clear?" Molly asked him sarcastically.

"Go with God," the priest said, bowing his head.

Molly drove a dilapidated Volkswagen Variant that had definitely seen better days. The toll of her driving, plus its age, caused the car to moan and groan even before it was started up. Now it took her three attempts before she could get it into reverse, and by that time they were halfway up the broad sweep of steps in front of the school. She finally got it pointed in the right direction and they took off in a flurry of gravel.

Perched as usual on the back of the driving seat was Mabel the parrot. Hennessy's parents had brought her back from Africa on their first leave some ten years before. She had had to spend six months in quarantine and, when she was finally rescued, she had become contrary to the point of galloping insanity. She hated everyone, and everyone hated her, but somewhere in her tiny brain she had worked out that if she attached herself to Molly she might be spared from extinction. This was what had happened, and from that time on the two of them had become inseparable. Strangely enough, over the years Molly had grown fond of her sullen companion and many's the time she had interceded on her behalf when the chopper was about to fall.

Hennessy sat as far away from Mabel as he could and stared out at the passing scenery. Now that he had achieved his objective of getting himself expelled, he'd have to start thinking about what the future might have in store for him. A return to Africa would be ideal: it was where he had spent most of his fifteen years of existence and he looked upon it more as his home than Ireland.

He had a fairly good idea, however, that that would be out of the question. His father was determined to have him educated in Ireland and he was just as stubborn as his son.

He gazed at his grandmother's bony profile and thought, not for the first time, how much she and the parrot were beginning to resemble one another. They both had the same hooked beak and beady eyes, and the old lady's brightly coloured, though old fashioned clothes, bore the same ruffled appearance as the bird's tattered plumage.

"So what're you going to do with me now?" Hennessy asked her, taking the plunge.

"I know what I'd like to do with you."

"What?"

"Put you in solitary confinement and throw away the key."

"You know that wouldn't work. I'm a master of escape. Houdini is my middle name."

"Is that so?"

Molly braked at a YIELD sign, then suddenly accelerated across the road. The driver of a Ford Transit van, which had been bowling merrily along, must have seen his life flash before him as he wrestled with the wheel to avoid hitting her.

"What's he blowing about?" Molly asked, glancing in the rear view mirror. "Some people think they own the road."

"You drove straight out in front of him."

"Hadn't I the right? There was a time when men would stand back to let women through. There's no manners any more."

"Manners any more," the parrot suddenly piped up. "Manners any more."

Hennessy gave up, then resuming their former conversation, he said, "You could send me back to Africa…"

"I could."

Encouraged, he went on, "That way I'd be out of your hair. I'd be someone else's problem then..."

"Your poor mother's, you mean?"

Sensing that he'd made a mistake, Hennessy sought to recover lost ground by proclaiming: "I'd be as good as gold if you sent me back. You know I like living with you and Pop...and Mabel," he added quickly, "but Africa is my real home. I've still got my return ticket...and my passport's in order..."

"Passport's in order," the parrot squawked. "Passport's in order..."

"You don't need a passport for the North Circular Road," Molly said grimly, "and that's where we're going. Mark my words, there'll be no going back to Africa until I've got you properly educated."

"Aw, come on, gran..."

"Don't you '*come on, gran*' with me, you scamp." Molly stuck her hand out the window to indicate that she was turning right, then she proceeded to turn left. A sharp blast on a horn told of another driver's outrage. "At great expense to your parents you were put in a perfectly good school and how d'you reward them? By getting yourself expelled, that's how. Now I've got to sit down and write to your father and explain to him how his son gummed up the works..."

"I didn't gum up the works. The opposite, as a matter of face. I got them running freely..."

His grandmother gave a snort of what sounded suspiciously like laughter. "Those poor boys..." she murmured, but she didn't sound particularly sorry for them.

"I felt hemmed in," Hennessy said, feeling that he owed her an explanation. "All those doors and locks and windows. In Africa everything was open to the sunlight. There were no rules and regulations…"

"You must have been like wild animals, yourself and your sister. And that reminds me, how is it that she's content in her school? Two years now she's been there and not a peep out of her. How is it she's been able to settle down and you haven't?"

In his mind's eye Hennessy saw his sister Alice, older by a year and quite the prim and proper little lady. She had never liked the strangeness of Africa, the smells, the heat, the mosquitoes. Running around in khaki shorts and shirt was not for her. She liked dressing up, having nice clothes, being in the company of other girls. Once she'd tried to dye her mosquito net pink. Mentally he curled a lip; being in a boarding school with a lot of other silly girls just suited her down to the ground.

"Well?" his grandmother prompted him. "Tell me how she's at her ease and you're not."

Hennessy hunted about for words but he knew it was a lost cause. His gran didn't want to listen. That was the trouble with adults, when they got an idea in their heads about what was good for you, it would take a stick of dynamite to shift it. His best course now would be to bide his time and hope that when he got on his grandparents' nerves sufficiently they'd come around to his way of thinking. In the meantime, he had the house in the North Circular Road with all its nooks and crannies and its huge jungle of a garden, to look forward to.

He looked at the road ahead and, as if to cheer him up, the sun came out. "The sun has got his hat on," he sang under his breath, "toora-loora-lay…" Then he turned to Mabel and stuck his tongue out at her.

2

The Caskeys lived in an old rambling house near the
Phoenix Park. It had been in Pop Caskey's family for
nearly a hundred and fifty years and the ravages of all
that time were plainly to be seen in its crumbling
brickwork and gap-tiled roof. Hennessy had a theory
that it was only the sucker-like veins of ivy which
webbed its walls that kept it from falling down.

Inside was a warren of rooms, old dark furniture
and staircases that creaked at night under the feet of
the ghosts of all the people who had lived there over
the years.

Hennessy loved it and its large unkempt gardens.
It was a place that gave full rein to his imagination.
When he was younger it had terrified him with
delight of the unknown: haunted rooms, unquiet
spirits, rattling chains, echoing footsteps that left no
prints behind on the dusty floors.

Now that he was older he was able to appreciate
its individuality, its uniqueness in the midst of all the
little boxes that builders were building and people
were living in because they had no choice in the
matter. He knew that his engineer father had tried to
persuade the old folk to sell it and move to a more
easily-managed house, and he was glad that they had

stubbornly refused even to consider such a move.

When he had his stuff safely stowed away in his attic room, Hennessy went up to Glasnevin Cemetery to see his grandfather. Pop was still very much in the land of the living, thin and bony like his wife but spry for all his seventy-odd years. He maintained that the graveyard was a sea of peace in the storm of life, but there was also the "hole-in-the-wall" arrangement with the public house that bordered the graveyard where he could have his morning glass of whiskey and pint of Guinness stout passed out to him without bothering to have to go inside.

Hennessy found him sitting in a sunny spot, his newspaper on his knees and his glasses perched on the end of his nose. At first he thought he was asleep but, when he drew near, Pop put up his hand and told him to keep quiet. He sat down carefully and strained his ears but for the life of him he couldn't hear anything.

After a time he said in a whisper, "What is it?"

"Listen," the old man said, "can't you hear him?"

"Who?"

"The willow-warbler. He's just back from his travels in the southern hemisphere."

Hennessy looked up into the trees.

"You mean that bird going crazy over there? He sounds as if he's got a thorn up his bum."

"Shame on you." Pop cocked his head into a listening attitude and a look of rapture came over his face. "Just think of the journey he's made to come back and sing to us. He's telling us that spring is in the air."

"So?"

"It means that I've made it through another winter. That's what he's telling me. Don't be careless of your youth, boy; it'll go soon enough."

"I wish I was grown up," Hennessy said moodily. "Then I could do what I wanted and not have everyone preaching at me. It's no fun being fifteen years old."

Pop looked at him over his glasses.

"You're right. I'll bet you've got the troubles of the world on your shoulders."

"There, you see, you don't take me seriously either. If I was your age you'd think every word that dropped from my lips was a jewel."

"No, I wouldn't. I'd think that you were another old fool like myself. The only jewels around here are the ones that bird is lilting into the air. And for that matter, what're you doing here anyway? Shouldn't you be in school?"

"I've been expelled."

"You haven't!"

"Oh, yes I have…"

"How did that come about?"

Hennessy recounted the story of his expulsion with some relish and, when he had finished, the old man laughed so hard his glasses fell off.

"By God, Mikey, that's a good one," he said between snorts. "That's the best one I've heard in a month of Sundays. What does your grandma think about that? I'll bet that's given her something to chew on."

"You can say that again. She's going up the walls. She tried to brain me with her handbag."

"Aha, it's hard to reason with an angry woman," Pop said, obviously speaking from experience. "You did right to get away from her until she's cooled down."

Hennessy picked a stem of grass and began moodily to chew it. It was pleasant sitting there with his back to the sun-warmed bricks of the wall. He could see why Pop liked the stillness and the quiet. No chance of the inhabitants of the place ticking you off for not washing the back of your neck, having your room tidy or getting up on time. Even the singing of the willow-warbler became bearable the more you listened to it. He began to build a fantasy in which himself and his grandfather camped out in the graveyard for the rest of the summer, living on berries and wild honey. They could dig the odd grave to make some money.

Pop broke in on his thoughts by asking him if he'd order the usual for him from Tom the barman: "Just beat a tattoo on the wall over there, three quick and three slow, and he'll stick his head out. Get yourself a lemonade or something stronger if you feel the need."

Hennessy did as he was bid and came back shortly carrying the drinks on a tin tray. It gave him a shudder of daring to be drinking in the midst of all the tombstones.

"What's that you've got there?" Pop asked him,

eyeing the drink he was holding.

"It's called a rock shandy. A mixture of orange and lemon…"

"Oh, well, bottoms." Pop raised his glass and the amber fluid glinted in the rays of the sun. "When we dead awaken," he toasted the graveyard at large, then he knocked the whiskey back in one swallow. Over his head his friend the willow-warbler was singing his heart out.

3

That was a Tuesday, and on Thursday over breakfast Molly told her grandson that she'd managed to get a new school for him: "It's a day school," she informed him. "No boarding this time. You'll be able to come home in the evenings so that I can keep an eye on you. We're going down this morning to meet the Principal, and if you so much as blink I'll have your guts for garters…"

Longingly Hennessy watched Pop make his usual escape but for him there was no way of avoiding what was in store for him. He was slightly surprised that Molly had managed to fix him up with a new school so quickly, especially if his reputation had gone before him. Maybe it was a reform school for young criminals?

Back in the Volkswagen, and with Mabel the parrot perched in her usual position, they drove down the North Circular, through Fairview and out along the coast road. It was another beautiful spring day, with the sun high up in a cloudless sky and a pleasant blare of heat radiating in through the windscreen. Hennessy's heart was still a wintry landscape, however, with forebodings of what was to come needling at him.

And the sight of the grey stone buildings of the school when they turned in did nothing to warm his thoughts. The cement yard was paper-littered and uneven and the bicycle shed was barricaded by iron bars that gave it the ominous look of a prison.

The main door had been defaced by some spray-painted graffiti and a fat individual in a flat cap was laboriously attempting to remove it. He was using a metal brush that left deep channels in the wood and the mess he was making looked worse than the graffiti.

Just as they came to the door a bell sounded stridently and they were immediately engulfed in a horde of pushing and shoving boys. At least Hennessy at first thought they were all boys, but then he noticed that a number of the laughing and swearing figures were undoubtedly girls. As they were all dressed in exactly the same fashion—runners, jeans and sweaters—it was easy to understand his mistake.

When the tide receded, Hennessy, Molly and the man with the brush were left cowering up against the wall. The man's bucket had been kicked over and a stream of soapy water was snaking its way forlornly towards the gutter.

The man let out a burst of profanity which if directed at the door would have burned the graffiti off it in one go. Then he noticed Molly, touched his cap and rolled his eyes to the heavens.

"I don't blame you," Molly told him. "They're like wild animals. And I've got another one of their like here for you to put up with."

They both gazed at Hennessy, Molly despairingly, the man with loathing. Under their scrutiny he shifted uneasily from foot to foot, thinking how unfair it was that he should get the blame for something he'd had no hand or part in. He was tempted to give the bucket an almighty kick, seeing as he was already being charged with knocking it over in the first place.

Still nursing his grievance, he was ushered in the door and along a paint-peeling corridor to the Principal's office. He turned out to be a small man wearing glasses and a shabby tweed suit. The most striking thing about him was his crown topper: it sat on top of his head, chestnut brown and gleaming, while the rest of the vegetation at the sides and at the back was badger-grey and liberally decorated with dandruff.

He avoided looking at Hennessy while he talked to Molly: "Yes, we have a place for the boy…In Form 4c," he muttered. "Only possible because one of their number left to take up a position as an apprentice butcher. A trial period, you understand." Mr House's eyes took on a faraway look as though he was visualising his ex-student attacking a side of beef.

"Yes," Molly prompted him.

"Ah, now what was I saying? Oh yes, we reserve the right of course to change our minds if he doesn't fit in…"

"Which?"

"I beg your pardon?"

"The apprentice butcher or my grandson?" Molly

asked, with a touch of exasperation.

Looking confused, Mr House said, "Well, whatever... Would he be capable of taking the Intermediate Certificate at the end of the present year? That would be a strike in his favour."

"Well, would you?" Molly said, giving Hennessy a nudge.

"Yes...What? Sure, of course..."

But Hennessy had switched off and was much more interested in what he could see outside the Principal's office. In the yard knots of students were standing about, laughing and talking. Trailing out from a number of the huddled groups he could see the tell-tale wisps of smoke that betokened the puffing of clandestine cigarettes. A girl with red hair was standing in profile talking to three or four boys who were smirking at whatever she was saying.

As he watched, the girl turned and looked in the window at him, catching his eye. She had a round, saucy face with a turned-up nose, and in the front her hair was streaked bright orange. She was wearing a black leather jacket, and a gold-coloured stud in her left ear lobe caught the sun. She looked tough and completely unlike the girls that his sister Alice sometimes brought to the house on the North Circular Road at holiday time.

Now, as he watched, she grinned at him, then made a rude, two-fingered gesture and Hennessy immediately felt his black mood begin to lift. Maybe this school wouldn't be such a pain in the gable-end after all.

Suddenly he became aware that the two people in the room with him were looking expectantly in his direction and he realised that he must have been asked a question.

"Sorry," he said, grinning inanely, "I didn't quite…"

"Oh, you…" Molly said, and for a moment he half expected her to make another swing at him with her handbag. "Mr House here has been wondering about books," she went on, "and I've asked him for a list. You've probably got most of them already…"

"Probably."

Molly turned back to Mr House.

"We're very grateful to you for taking him in," she said. "And at such short notice. Now I can write to my poor daughter out in Africa and put her mind at rest. She'll be so pleased…"

I don't know about that, Hennessy thought, looking out the window again to where the red-haired girl now had her tongue stuck out and her eyes crossed. But even if his mother mightn't be too happy about his new place of education, he himself felt a ripple of anticipation. Things were definitely looking up.

4

St Jude's on a Monday morning mirrored the bad-tempered humour of four hundred students hung over from a weekend of freedom. There was no jollity, no shouted greetings: most classes filed dutifully into their classrooms, only the closest of friends being able to dredge up tired smiles at the sight of one another. Even the teachers seemed down-in-the-mouth, as though they were being forced to go to school just like their charges.

Hennessy was put in Form 4c and sat in a desk beside a fat boy called Brooks, who confided to him in a stage whisper that he was the champion farter of the class. The room was high-ceilinged and had enormous arched windows that creaked in their frames in the March wind. The walls were painted a kind of sick green and the clock over the blackboard had stopped, its hands paralysed at five minutes to four.

The first lesson was Mathematics, taught by a stocky, hard-looking man with close-cropped hair. His name was Lawless. It only took him a moment or two to spot that Hennessy was new to the class.

"Another blow-in, I see," he said, squinting as though Hennessy's appearance caused him pain.

"From what den of iniquity have you crawled? And what crime did you commit to get your walking papers?"

Hennessy raised his eyebrows, but said nothing.

"You refuse to answer?"

"Sir?"

"I asked you where you've come from."

"The North Circular Road, Dublin 7, via Africa."

"What school, you ludramawn?"

"Assisi College."

"Ah, one of the quality. Why'd you leave?"

"I was asked to."

"Expelled?"

"Yes, sir."

"And of course our bleeding heart of a principal took you in..."

"No sir, my grandmother took him in."

There was a pause, with the whole class holding its collective bated breath, but Lawless decided to let that one pass.

"What's your name?" he went on, only a tightening of the lips betraying his displeasure.

"Hennessy, sir. Michael Hennessy."

"Well, Hennessy, my name is Lawless. Mr Lawless, but nicknamed 'The Judge'"—there was a titter in the class—"and as well as endeavouring to teach you mathematics I'm also the form master of this lovely bunch of layabouts you see before you. You'll find me just but merciless. I'm a man of peace but if you cross me I'll bite off your nose and eat it. Get my drift?"

Hennessy stared him out; then, as his eyes began to water, he slowly raised them until he was gazing at the ceiling. It was composed of fibreglass panels, and one of them kept rising and falling as the wind blew. In a moment the rest of the class had raised their eyes; then Mr Lawless followed suit. There was a silence.

"What in God's name are you looking at?" the teacher finally asked, a frown furrowing his face.

"It's the ceiling, sir."

"I know it's the ceiling, but why are you looking at it?"

"No particular reason, sir."

The titter ran around the class again and Lawless's face flushed with anger. But suddenly he smiled. "So," he said, "we've got ourselves a smart aleck. A bit of a boyo. Is that what you are, Hennessy, a bit of a boyo?"

"If you say so, sir."

"I do say so. And what's more I'm going to keep my eye on you. And to start you off on the right foot, as it were, I'd like you to write out the sentence: 'I must not gaze at the ceiling during maths class,' one hundred times. And have it for me by Wednesday. Have you got that? Is that clear to you, boy?"

Under his breath Hennessy muttered, "As clear as muddy water," but aloud he said, "Yes, sir. One hundred times, sir. By Wednesday, sir. I must not gaze at the ceiling during maths class."

There was a break at 10.45, and everyone trotted,

sauntered or galloped out into the yard. Two teachers walked up and down, keeping a wary eye out for trouble, but they made no attempt to delve into the various nooks and corners where most of the students huddled.

Hennessy stood with Brooks, but upwind of him in case he decided to prove his prowess with his rear end. A pimply-faced boy of about his own age came over and said. "That was a nice one, head. The ceiling bit. You had the Judge going there for a minute."

Hennessy shrugged, looking pleased.

"My name's Swift," the boy said. "Call me Swifty. You got a fag?"

"A cigarette?"

"That's it. A gasper. A coffin-nail. You light one end, blow smoke out the other. You know what I'm talking about doncha?"

"I do. But I haven't got one. I don't use them."

"Not to worry."

Swift made a gesture with his arm as though he was shaking something off his hand, and immediately a rather battered-looking cigarette appeared between his fingers. Nonchalantly he flipped it into his mouth.

"Hey," Brooks said appreciatively.

Swift cocked an eyebrow; then, with his other hand he ran a match along the wall and set fire to the cigarette. Smoke dribbled out his nose.

"Good trick that, Swifty," Brooks said.

"You think so?"

"Like that magician guy on the telly: Paul Daniels..."

"Like that magician guy on the telly," Swift said, mimicking Brooks. He turned to Hennessy. "You wanna watch out for old Brooksie. He doesn't drink, smoke, curse or go with girls. Proper mammie's boy. And he's fat, fat, fat..."

They both gazed at Brooks, who went red with embarrassment. He was very fat, his round pudding face soft and lardy, his eyes like two shiny stuck-on raisins.

Swift smoked his cigarette in a professional cupped hand, the lighted end turned inward and, when one of the parading teachers drew near, he put the hand in his pocket, pursed his lips and began to whistle cheerfully. He had spiky blond hair and the beginnings of a moustache on his upper lip, the hairs of which could just about be counted. He was dressed completely in black and, when he turned sideways, Hennessy could see the words *The Cure* stencilled in brass studs on the back of his jacket.

"So what's the scene?" Swift asked when the teacher had moved on. "How'd you get yourself expelled from this Assisi College? You set fire to the place or what?

Hennessy told him and Swift laughed. So did Brooks, a high pitched, fluting neigh. Swift frowned at him and Brooks broke off in the middle, his mouth closing with an audible snap.

"Who told you you could laugh?" Swift asked him. "Did I? Did Henno here?"

Miserably Brooks shook his head. Hennessy felt sorry for him but he was so pleased at being called

Henno that he said nothing. Swift looked like someone whose friendship should be cultivated; he seemed hard and knowing. Brooks, on the other hand, appeared like one of life's victims, someone to be teased, made fun of and tormented. Still, he was the first boy to have spoken to Hennessy in St Jude's, and for that he was grateful.

The bell to call them back to class sounded and they moved, only more slowly this time. Hennessy gazed about him, hoping to catch sight of the red-haired girl he'd seen from the Principal's office. She didn't appear to be about the place, however.

Later on that morning Form 4c had a free period because a teacher was absent. Mr House came in and gave them some work to do; then wandered away and left them to their own devices. Immediately a commotion broke out, with a rising tide of voices and pieces of chewed paper flying around the room. There were only six girls in the class, and they sat together and pretended to ignore the rowdiness of their male companions.

Because most of the paper pellets seemed directed at Brooks, Hennessy, sitting beside him, had to defend himself with a copybook held in front of his face. Tiring of that, he took a rubber band, wound it round his thumb and index finger and began to flick some projectiles of his own at their tormentors. Soon a major battle was in progress, with the people at his side of the room joining him against the others. Even Brooks half-heartedly threw a few pellets.

Hennessy, busily aiming a juicy bomb at Swift on the other side of the room, suddenly became aware that a silence had descended on the class. He looked up and saw Mr Lawless standing just inside the door and staring straight at him. The fright he got caused him instinctively to let go of the taut rubber band, and the pulpy missile whizzed across the room, missed Lawless's head by a fraction and splattered against the wall behind him.

There was an intake of breath from the class, and Hennessy felt as if he had been hit in the back of the head by the proverbial lump of black pudding. He could already hear the accusation from an irate Molly: "Only a day in the place and you almost take the head off the form teacher!" This could be the quickest expulsion since Adam was thrown out of the Garden of Paradise.

Lawless went purple in the face and took on the appearance of someone who was about to choke. Through gritted teeth he managed to squeeze out, "Who threw that?"

There was a silence so deep that it could almost be heard. Everyone's head was down, fingers busily writing. This was a class obviously very serious about its work.

Lawless was not to be fooled. "Pens down," he commanded. "Fold your arms. We're going to get to the bottom of this if it takes till doomsday."

He went to the top of the room and gazed about him, but no one would meet his eye. "If the culprit doesn't own up within one minute," he said, "I'll give the whole class a punishment exercise that'll have you writing until your fingers fall off. Now, what's it to be? One execution or a bloody massacre...?"

Heads began to turn in Hennessy's direction and he was about to do the right thing when, to his amazement, Brooks stood up and said, "It was me, sir. But it was a mistake. I wasn't trying to hit you."

Lawless looked at him, and so did the rest of the class, most of them with their mouths open. Hennessy was having none of it and made to stand up, but found that he was immobilised by Brooks holding a handful of his sweater.

"I'm very sorry, sir," Brooks went on, a quaver in his voice. "I don't know what got into me. It was just that everyone was throwing things at me and I couldn't stand it any longer."

"Humph," Lawless said, "I know the feeling. Still, I have to give you credit for owning up. See me after class and we'll work out what I'm going to do with you. And if I hear another sound from this room, I won't be responsible for what I'll do..."

"Thank you, sir."

But the enormity of what he had done must have suddenly hit Brooks, and the relief of getting off lightly expressed itself in a way that was probably typical. Brooks farted...

5

Brooks was the hero of the hour. At the lunch break, and again after school, guys and girls kept coming up to him and congratulating him on what he had done. Even Swift grudgingly admitted that he had done something worthwhile after all.

They were in the shop-cum-café across the road from the school. It was called Nixers and was presided over by an evil-looking old man with a stutter and, although this was only rumoured, a wooden leg. He answered to the name of Robert, but most people referred to him as Bad Bob. He was also rumoured to have eyes in the back of his head, for no one had ever been known to lift anything from the shop. He was usually in a vile humour, grumpy, scowling and with an habitual expression on his face that would turn milk sour.

Hennessy, being the newcomer and in funds, bought cans of Coke and packets of crisps for Brooks, Swift and a friend of Swift's called Nedser O'Brien. The place was packed, everyone was smoking and you could cut the atmosphere with a blunt knife.

Shouting to be heard above the din, Swift asked Hennessy what kind of music he liked.

"I dunno, I'm not really into that scene. Frank

Sinatra? Ella Fitzgerald?"

"That's real cool, man. Anybody can like 'The Sisters of Mercy' or 'Motorhead'. Takes a real dude to appreciate old lags like them."

"Have I said the wrong thing?"

"No, honest to God and scratch me, Momma, with a downbeat. What about 'Songs for Swinging Lovers'?"

"What about them?"

"Way out..."

"You're having me on."

O'Brien finished his Coke and put the empty can on the counter. Then he began shaking his head violently and playing an imaginary guitar.

"What's up with him?" Hennessy asked, looking at him with alarm.

"He's moshing."

"What?"

"It's called moshing. Where've you been, head? Come down in the last shower or what? You must be some kind of alien..."

"A spacer," O'Brien mumbled, breaking off his St Vitus dance. "Hey man, you dig the alternative scene? Goths, Punks, Neo-Hippies...?"

"Pardon?"

"Where it's at, like. All human life, like in the *News of the World*. Listen we're trying to get a group together. D'you strum an engine, beat the tom-toms, knock out some vibes on the synthesiser?"

"I'm lost," Hennessy said, shaking his head. "You'll have to translate for me."

"He's asking you if you play a musical instrument," Swift said. "He's been trying to get a group together since he saw Meatloaf sweat."

"What d'you think we should call it, Swifty?" O'Brien inquired, the eyes starting out of his head.

"Call what?"

"You know, the group..."

"How about Vomit and the Pukers?"

"Very funny. But you'll be sorry when I'm raking in the mega-bucks. Up there on that neon-lit stage in front of millions of groupies, all of them trying to pull my trousers off."

"That'll be the day."

They went outside and stood looking up and down the road. A thin April wind was blowing in from the estuary, carrying on its breath the smell of dank seaweed and sewage. The school buildings looked drab and forlorn and empty of their accustomed life. Only Harry the caretaker moved about in the yard, picking up scraps of paper and other debris.

"Time to head for the gaff," Swift said. His face was pinched and white from the cold, and his spots stood out as though he'd been picking at them. "I've a ton of homework to do. Don't know why I bother. The first chance I get, I'm gone..."

"What'll you do?" Hennessy asked, genuinely curious.

"Join the army, maybe. Or take the boat. Two of my brothers are in London. On the buildings. They're making a fortune."

"Nah, don't mind him," O'Brien broke in. "You

should hear him on the drums. Can he make that pigskin sing. He and me'll be up there in the big leagues just as soon a we get our act together."

"When'll that be, Nedser?"

"First Sunday in Bray if I've anything to say about it."

"Say about it!" Swift muttered, suddenly looking angry. "What've you to say about it? We should be so lucky. The music business is all sewn up. It's a question of who you know, just like everything else. All these new groups are made of upper-class twits who go around preaching about saving the trees and the flowers and the whales... If you have an address like ours, you haven't a chance."

"Aw, there you go again," O'Brien said, shaking his head. "You know what you are, you're a pessimist..."

"Will I tell you the definition of a pessimist?" Brooks suddenly interjected. "He's the guy who looks at his pint of stout and sees that it's half gone. The optimist, on the other hand, sees that half of it is left..."

The other three looked at him, then in unison they groaned.

"So, how was school?" Hennessy's grandmother asked him when he got home.

Molly was out at the back of the house in her workroom painting a large canvas that she had spread out on the ground. She was wearing overalls and gloves, and her hair was caught up in a brightly-coloured scarf.

"Okay," Hennessy said.

"Only okay?"

He sidled around trying to get a glimpse of what she was doing.

"I got into a bit of trouble..."

"Oh, no." Molly groaned, pausing in her work. "What'd you do now?"

"Nothing very much. The master thought I was being cheeky, so he gave me some lines to do."

"On your first day..."

Hennessy shrugged, regretting his honesty. He should have said that everything in the garden was lovely. "What're you doing?" he asked, as much to change the subject as to satisfy his curiosity.

"I'm painting a sign."

"I can see that. But what's it about?"

"It's for the Anti-Bloodsports League. There's a coursing meeting at the weekend that we're going to picket."

"I didn't know you were into that."

"Well, I am."

Molly was an ardent campaigner: ecology, nuclear power-stations, the status of women, you name it, she was into it. Each cause was like a fence that she had to jump, and quite often she came a cropper so that she was forever in and out of courthouses. So far she had managed to stay out of gaol, but only just.

Hennessy cast his eye critically over the sign. It showed two greyhounds in pursuit of a hare. The dogs were huge, with slavering jaws and red rimmed eyes, while the hare was small, terrified and badly in need of a good feed. Underneath Molly had scrawled, in lurid green letters, the words *Bullyboys at Work*.

"What d'you think?" she asked, absentmindedly scratching her head with the handle of the paint brush.

"Very good. I didn't know you were so talented. You should do a few more and hold an exhibition. What was the name of that old dame who became a famous painter in her seventies...?"

"Grandma Moses."

"That's the one. You could be Grandma Caskey, the Irish version."

"Don't be so sarcastic. It's a pity you wouldn't get involved in some worthy cause. It'd be good for your soul. Maybe stop you getting into trouble."

"What're you saying?" Hennessy was outraged. "You'll probably get arrested. I've heard of the goings-on of those people. They even plant bombs..."

"They do not."

"Oh, yes, they do. They cause damage, break into scientific research stations and release all the animals..."

"Have you seen what they do to the animals in those places?"

"I don't think I want to know, especially not before I've had my dinner."

"Well, there you are then."

Molly stuck the paintbrush into a jar of white spirit; then took off her gloves. There was a smear of green paint across her nose. Mabel the parrot, who had been roosting in the rafters, suddenly roused herself and flew down and perched on Molly's shoulder. She opened her beak and began to tear at Molly's coloured scarf.

"Why don't you send Mabel in for a scientific examination?" Hennessy asked artfully. "That report should make for interesting reading. They might find out what makes her so contrary all the time."

Molly frowned. "Mabel is a most sweet-tempered bird," she said. "You probably torment her when my back is turned."

The bird had succeeded in unwinding the cloth and was now busily engaged in tearing it into pieces. It made an odd, grating sound as it worked, as though it was grinding whatever teeth it had.

"Yes, just look at her," Hennessy agreed. "That could be just as well your ear that she's munching on."

"Nonsense."

The bird let go of the scarf and began hopping up and down on Molly's shoulder.

This time it was Hennessy's turn to frown. "What's wrong with her now?" he inquired.

"She's hungry. It's past her dinner time."

"Ditto with me. What're we having?"

"Caskey"—Molly always referred to her husband by his surname—"is making it. It's his turn."

"Oh, no," Hennessy groaned, "that means burned stew... It'll be stuck to the pot and I'll have to clean it. Not to mention having to eat the stew itself."

"You poor boy..."

"Now who's being sarcastic?"

"Maybe for once he won't burn it."

"Yes, and maybe Mabel'll come down and kiss my you know what..."

The bird glared at Hennessy. It had a nasty way of working its mouth that made Hennessy feel that a strategic retreat was in order. That razor-sharp beak could do ferocious damage to whatever it came in contact with—like his nose, for instance.

6

Wednesday was games day in St Jude's and most of the student body was obliged to take part in some form of recreation. Hennessy elected to go for soccer, simply because Swift and O'Brien were doing so. Brooks felt that chess more suitably fitted his size and shape.

They togged out in one of the classrooms and it was soon obvious to Hennessy that not everyone subscribed to the routine of a weekly bath.

"Phew," he said holding his nose, "it certainly pongs in here."

"Yeah, a crowd of boggers," Swift agreed. He picked up one of O'Brien's socks and sniffed daintily at it. "Definitely dead since last Tuesday week," he pronounced. "Dead but it won't lie down."

"Aw, gimme that."

O'Brien grabbed the sock and began to pull it on. Dried mud, caked on it, spattered all over the floor. The sock was so rotten that the top parted from the foot, and O'Brien fell backwards out of the desk and ended up on his head and with his legs in the air.

They had to carry their boots with them and put them on outside the door. A fine drizzle was sifting down from a grey sky and the yard was slick and dangerously slippery. One of the more boisterous members of Form 4c was already being led back in with two badly grazed knees.

As they did up their laces Hennessy said to Swift, "There was a girl...Eh, I saw her last week when I was being interviewed by Housey. Through his window..."

"You were being interviewed through Housey's window?"

"No, you cabbage head, I saw her through the window."

"Oh, yeah?"

"Who was she?"

"How do I know? There must be a hundred birds in St Jude's. Describe her."

"Well, she had red hair. With an orange streak in the front. Had on a black jacket. It's just..."—Hennessy was beginning to feel sorry that he'd started now— "Well, it's just that I haven't seen her around," he finished lamely. "Doesn't matter..."

"Sounds like Liz Finn," Swift said, pursuing it. "She's out on work experience. Learning to be a hairdresser. Liz is a nutter. Do anything to be noticed. You interested?"

"What d'you mean?"

"You going to try putting the shift on her?"

"I might. If I knew what it meant..."

"Best be careful with her. Wear protective clothes, like a suit of armour for instance. She's Mad Max's bird..."

"Who?"

"Mad Max Bacon, the king of the Goths."

They went out through the school gates; then waited at the traffic lights for the little green man to appear. O'Brien, too impatient to wait, began weaving in and out through the speeding traffic.

"The lemoner," Swift said, looking anxiously after him, "he's for the chop if he slips under one of those chariots."

But he was still alive and well and merely breathing heavily when they made it to the far side. "You should never've let go of your old dear's apron strings," Swift told him.

"Why?"

"You could'a been killed. Joined old Jim Reeves and Elvis the Pelvis in that big gig in the sky."

"You worried about me, Swifty?"

"You think that, you've got a hole in your head. I just didn't fancy the job of scraping you off the road."

The playing-pitches were part of the public park and a footpath ran through the one that they elected to play on. Swift counselled Hennessy to go for that one because the teacher refereeing hadn't a clue: "Fats Barlow doesn't want to be out here no more than we do," he said. "He just goes through the motions. We can do what we like."

They played for a while and Hennessy scored a goal. Swift was good, quick and fast and with excellent ball control. It was he who gave the pass that enabled Hennessy to score. O'Brien kept falling over his own feet, and it didn't help that the boots he was wearing were as ancient and falling-apart as his socks.

"Come on, come on," Swift kept nagging him, "You'll never get picked for Italy on that form."

They took a breather while the ball was down the other end of the pitch and Swift lit a cigarette. "So, who's this Mad Max Bacon then?" Hennessy asked. A cheer went up as Fats fell over on his back in a puddle.

"He's in Form 4d. Thick as elephant crap but strong as an ox. I once saw him hold up a car while a mate of his robbed the wheel."

"You're kiddin'"

"Well, only a teeny bit. But you wouldn't want to get involved with Maxie. He's heap bad medicine."

"I'll watch out for him."

"You won't have much trouble seeing him. He's as wide across as he is long and a spanner to boot."

"A spanner?"

"He's got crossed eyes. One looks east, the other looks west, and Max is a candidate for the cuckoo's nest."

"He must be something to see."

"He's a corker."

There was a rumpus at the other end of the field and O'Brien, who was beginning to look like a mudman from all the times he'd fallen over, said, "Hey look at that. Those Hoodies are after robbin' our football..."

Swift took a last pull from his cigarette and stamped it out. Four characters wearing silver-coloured tracksuits and with the hoods pulled up were running across the field kicking the football and yelling. After them in a posse came most of the two teams, with Fats Barlow bringing up the rear like a winded water-buffalo.

"They're looking for a chase," Swift shouted. "Let's go."

With a whoop he took off, running diagonally to cut off the interlopers. Hennessy ran beside O'Brien, between gasps asking him who these people were.

"They're mashers," he replied. "Always out for trouble. If you go down their area with two ears and no broken nose they call you a sissy..."

The three of them got in front of the Hoodies, who paused, allowing the rest of the footballers to catch up. They formed a ring, with the toughs in the middle. Fats was still some way behind, shouting, "I say, I say..."

The Hoodies were quite young, not more than twelve or thirteen. One of them dropped the football on the ground and put his foot on it. The other three took up martial arts stances, legs bent, hands in the chopping position.

Swift, who appeared to have elected himself leader of the good guys, began circling round, his head thrust forward, a ferocious scowl on his face. After an interval of showing himself off silently, he mouthed, "Okay, Silkas, let's have our property back. Give it up, walk away, and you get to keep your marriage prospects..."

"Nah," one of the Hoodies snarled, but then inspiration seemed to desert him. He looked around at the ring of faces, all of them plainly showing that no mercy need be expected.

Fats had caught up by now and was vainly trying to push his way through the crowd. "No fighting now, boys," he bleated. "Just get the ball back. That's all we want, just the ball..."

The fellow with his foot on it suddenly bent and picked it up and kicked it straight at Swift. Immediately there was a yell from the assembled mob and the Hoodies, Swift and Fats were engulfed. Hennessy was pushed forward and found himself confronting one of the enemy, a wiry individual with a snarling mouth and yellow teeth. Before he could bring his hands up to defend himself he received a blow in the eye that caused a glorious burst of fireworks to explode in front of his vision. He would have fallen over except for the crowd pushing him from behind. The surge carried him right on through and out the other side, leaving him alone and pale and nursing his injured eye.

The mêlée steamrolled down a grassy bank, with everyone sliding and slipping and cursing. At one stage Fats appeared, like Moby Dick coming up for air, then he disappeared again into the seething mass. The football, forgotten, was left in the middle of the pitch, until two small boys came along, picked it up, and ran off with it.

Overhead, the skies suddenly opened and a great whoosh of rain beat down, as though someone up there wished to dampen the ardour of the combatants. In the confusion, the Hoodies broke free, and took off into the sheets of rain, but no one gave chase.

Honour had been satisfied, although it didn't seem to occur to anyone that the prize, namely the football, had been lost.

"My God, what happened to your eye?"

Hennessy's grandmother gazed at him in shock and horror, her mouth open. Even the parrot perched on her shoulder seemed overcome by the splendour of Hennessy's shiner.

"It's a long story, Molly," Hennessy responded, feeling so sorry for himself that he would gladly have stretched out on the linoleum floor of the kitchen and gone straight to sleep.

"You'd better get some raw meat on it," Molly advised him, moving to the refrigerator and taking out a lump of steak. The Parrot made a grab at it, and for a moment it was touch and go as to who would win out. In the end Molly claimed the victory and handed the meat to Hennessy.

"What'll I do with it? he asked, looking doubtfully at it with his one good eye.

"Put it on your eye. It'll draw out the pain and the bruising."

"Are you sure?"

"Well it's supposed to. How'd you get it anyway?"

Hennessy began to tell her about the incident on the playing field, then changed his mind and merely said that he'd got an elbow into the face in a football match. The other story was too open to misinterpretation.

When he'd finished Molly sighed, then she took

a closer look at his injury. "It'll be black and blue in the morning," she told him, "But I don't think there's any need to call the doctor. You'll suffer worse before you're twice married."

"I think I'll go and lie down for a while. I've got a bit of a headache. If one of the teachers, a Mr Barlow, rings to see if I'm all right, tell him I am."

Hennessy went up the stairs feeling as if he'd just stepped through the pain barrier. Life in St Jude's was certainly turning out to be eventful...

7

It was Saturday morning, and the birds were going mad outside Hennessy's window. He lay in his sleeping bag and listened to them, while the sun streamed in and warmed the room.

The sleeping bag was a habit he'd got into in Africa to keep the bugs out, and now he couldn't sleep anywhere else. Once he snuggled into it at night he felt safe and protected and free from the cares of the world.

After a time he crawled out and went over to the window. Spring was well into its stride and the cherry blossom trees in the garden were frosted with white and pink curls. His eye throbbed a little but the swelling had gone down and the purple bruising had faded to a dirty shade of grey.

All in all, he was feeling pretty pleased with himself. He wouldn't admit it to Molly but he had settled in at St Jude's, had made some friends, was not too much at odds with the teachers. There was a relaxed atmosphere about the place, a feeling of live and let live. If you did a little work, minded your own business and abided by the few rules and regulations that were in force then no one would say boo to you. Little was seen of Mr House, the Principal; it was rumoured that he'd had a tunnel dug from his office to the carpark and that when the school settled down at nine o'clock he made use of it to go home, only to reappear at four to lock up.

Swift and O'Brien had managed to get two other fellows to join them to form a group and they were due to give their first gig in a fortnight's time. Hennessy had sat in on one or two of their rehearsals and to his untutored ear they sounded flash and loud enough to wake the dead.

He got into his clothes and went downstairs. Pop Caskey was sitting reading a newspaper in the kitchen. He was wearing shorts and a wide-brimmed straw hat. Pop was a physical fitness fiend and did an hour of jerks and knee bends every morning and evening of his life. It was not unusual to meet him walking about on his hands, and Hennessy in his time had come across a useful amount of money fallen periodically from his grandfather's upturned pockets. Although now in his seventieth year, he was as fit as a man half his age.

A mountain of used crockery was teetering in the kitchen sink and the smell of burning toast filled the room.

"Cripes," Hennessy said, pulling the blackened bread out from under the grill. "The house could be burning down around you, Pop, and you'd be sitting there in the middle of it reading your newspaper or paring your toe nails."

"What?"

"The toast... you've let it burn."

"Oh dear, I forgot all about it."

Pop didn't look in the least repentant. "Listen to this," he said, rustling his paper. "A fellow up in Cavan found a chalice dating back a couple of thousand years. Just dug into the side of a hill and there it was. Just shows you what these yokes can do..."

The "yoke" that he was referring to was a metal detector, one of which he had purchased recently. For the last week he had been trotting up and down the garden, looking as if he was being pulled along by the buzzing metal stick. The results of his labours could be seen in one corner as a pile of old tin cans, a poker, a car battery and a rusted kettle. Molly spoke of it sarcastically as Pop's treasure trove.

Hennessy put two more slices of bread under the grill; then he boiled the kettle and made tea.

"Have some Rice Krispies," Pop said. "They go snap, crackle and pop."

"I know that."

The old man put down his paper and looked at his grandson. "What're you so grumpy about?" he asked him. "On such a morning as this..."

"You're not going to tell me to listen to the willow-warbler again, are you?"

"You could do worse."

Hennessy gestured at the pile of delf in the sink. "I'm not grumpy," he said. "It's just that the mess in this kitchen puts me off."

"What mess? That's just ordered disorder."

Neither Molly nor Pop had any idea how to run a

house, both of them being too preoccupied with the things that interested them, Molly with her causes, Pop with his fitness programme and the knick-knacks that he bought or invented. Most of the time Hennessy admired them and their determination to live life to the full but as it invariably was left to him to do the cleaning he became irritable with them from time to time.

He sat down at the table, poured some tea, buttered the toast. "You want some?" he offered, "or do you just like it burnt?"

"I'll have a fresh cup of tea." Pop pushed his straw hat to the back of his head. His face, hands and arms were already tanned from the spring sun. "Burnt toast is good for you," he said conversationally. "We used to clean our teeth with ashes once upon a time. And chew tar when it melted on the road."

"Oh yeah? Pull the other one."

"Honest to God. It was our chewing gum and it lasted all day."

"Tar?"

Pop put three spoonfuls of sugar in his tea and stirred it thoughtfully. "Did you ever have fried bread? Now that was something on a cold winter's morning. Fried in bacon fat. I was brought up on it..."

"Didn't make you grow very tall," Hennessy said critically.

"I was six foot two in my prime. As you grow older you shrink."

"D'you think I'll grow tall?"

"You should. Your father's a tall man. And that

reminds me, there's a letter for you."

"From my father?"

"No, from your mother."

"Oh."

Hennessy took the letter and stuffed it in his pocket, avoiding Pop's eye.

"Aren't you going to read it?"

"Later." Hennessy made a face. "I know what's in it, anyhow. She'll just be giving out to me. That's what mothers seem to be best at..."

"That's not fair. She's worried about you, and it just expresses itself as giving out. You should write to her, tell her you like your new school, that you've settled in..."

"I will, Pop, I will," Hennessy promised. "This weekend, definitely..."

Pop had gone out to trail his metal detector round the garden and Hennessy was just finishing washing up when his grandmother breezed in. She was wearing a long black coat and something like an upside down bird's nest was perched on her head.

"Oh, are you done?" she asked him, surveying the new neatness of the kitchen.

"Why, were you coming to help me?"

"No, not really. I've got a million things to do."

Mabel flew in after her and alighted on the towel rail. She fluffed her feathers, then began to peck under her wing.

"Look at that filthy bird," Hennessy said. "She's full of fleas."

"Nonsense, that bird is as clean as I am."

Mabel cawed, lifted her leg and deposited her droppings on the floor. To add insult to injury, she then gave a satisfied grunt as though to signify a job well done.

Hennessy snapped the dishcloth at her and she rose up in the air with a shriek. She flew to the top of a cupboard and huddled there, glaring down at him.

"There, now you've frightened her," Molly said. "She's got a very sensitive nature, you know."

"Sensitive nature my foot," Hennessy said furiously. "She's about as sensitive as a plank of wood."

"There now," Molly coaxed him. "Don't worry about it. I'll clean up after her."

"It's not just the mess, it's the principle of the thing."

"What d'you mean?"

"She did that deliberately because she knew I'd cleaned up."

"That's ridiculous..."

"No, it's not. That bird is evil. She's possessed by the devil."

"So, what d'you want to do, have her burned at the stake?"

Hennessy looked at his grandmother and started to grin. Molly raised her eyebrows at him; then she too laughed. "Or maybe I should send for the priest," she said, "and have him come and pray over her?"

"She'd certainly turn his hair grey."

Obviously changing the subject, Molly said, "Well,

I'm off on picket duty. Why don't you come with me? Do your bit for our animal friends."

"I've got my friend Brooks coming over. We were going to try out Pop's metal detector."

"You'll be lucky. He won't leave it out of his hands. He's hoping to find Fionn MacCumhaill's breast-plate or Cormac MacAirt's crown. Your friend could come along as well, the more the merrier."

Hennessy thought about it. It was a beautiful day and a trip down the country certainly had its attractions. "Won't it be dangerous?" he asked Molly. "Those blood sports people might like the taste of the human kind for a change."

"Not at all," Molly said airily. "It's a peaceful protest. We'll merely walk up and down with our banners. We're not going to interfere with anyone."

"Supposing they set their dogs on us?"

"They won't do that; they've too much regard for the beasts. It's only the poor defenceless hares that they torment."

"I'll see what Brooks says."

Molly shrugged. "I'm leaving in half an hour. Bring your wellingtons if you're coming."

She went out, the bird in her wake. It was only after she'd gone that Hennessy realised that she'd neglected to clean up the mess on the floor.

8

It was indeed a glorious spring day. They went up through the Phoenix Park, its broad open spaces hazy with sunshine, then out on to the Navan Road and into Meath. Easter lambs, oblivious of their fate, dawdled in lush meadows and a young colt kicked up his heels as he chased his shadow up the slope of a hill.

Brooks was intrigued with Mabel and kept trying to get her to talk: "Pretty Polly, pretty Polly," he repeated over and over in a falsetto voice that grated on Hennessy's nerves.

Finally he told him, "Will you shut up, you idiot. You sound like one of those toy birds you see outside sweet shops. If I put a penny in your slot, will you drop a chewing gum in my hand?"

"Aw, I just wanted to hear him say something," Brooks protested.

"You might be sorry...And it's not a him; it's a her."

Molly drove along narrow country roads at a breakneck pace, the back of the car slewing around corners, the wheels skidding. She was hunched forward, her nose an inch from the windscreen, her silly hat tilted sideways on her head.

Brooks, holding on for dear life, nodded in her direction. "Does she always drive like this?" he whispered. "Or is she going for a new land speed record?"

"She used to be a racing driver," Hennessy explained with a poker face. "Disguised herself as a man and almost won the world championship..."

"And I suppose the parrot was the navigator?"

Hennessy winked. "Not too many people know that," he said.

Wishing to avoid publicity, the coursing people had changed venue a number of times but the anti-bloodsports pickets were as dogged as a pack of income-tax inspectors. Molly joined a convoy of cars and jeeps that was winding its way down a muddy lane. Soon they were stopped by a policeman who was looking decidedly hot and harassed. He ordered them to back up but the congestion was such that they were soon bogged down, able to go neither forward nor back.

Everyone got out, and a large woman and a small man attempted to put some order on the protesters. "Women and children to the front," the woman commanded. "Men at the back. That way they won't charge us."

The little man scurried up and down the line of marchers, his hat, eyes and nose showing his anxiety, for all the world like an eager terrier ready to nip at their heels.

"Is he her husband?" Brooks asked Hennessy.

"No, he's her lunch."

They started forward, banners held aloft. Someone began half-heartedly to sing, "We Shall Overcome," but it died when it was discovered that no one knew the words. Molly's sign was bigger than anyone else's and Brooks and Hennessy had to help her to hold it up.

The field where the coursing was to take place was just that—a field. There was a waist-high hedge with a gap in it. This gap was manned by two burly characters in belted overcoats and wellington boots. They looked grim, determined and tough.

The large woman marched up to them and soon they were abusing one another at the tops of their voices. The crowd, pressing from behind, began forcing them backwards and suddenly they broke ranks and stampeded into the field. The coursing had already begun and a hare flew past, pursued by two greyhounds. Immediately the little man took off after them and some joker shouted, "Two to one the man in the hat."

There was pandemonium as the protesters and the coursing people came face to face. Blows were exchanged, children cried, women screamed. Molly's sign, filled like a sail by a gust of wind, bore Hennessy and Brooks forward, their feet barely touching the ground. They were on a collision course with a van with a loudspeaker on its roof when the wind changed direction and they started back-pedalling. Brooks fell over, leaving Hennessy on his own, but he soon decided that enough was enough and he let go of the banner. The last he saw of it, it was disappearing into the sky like a kite, weaving crazily from side to side and making strange, whooshing sounds.

"This is great, isn't it?" Brooks beamed, appearing again at Hennessy's side. "I wouldn't have missed this for the world."

They paused to survey the scene. Some of the protesters had succeeded in releasing the caged hares and they were hopping all over the place, their backsides in the air. The greyhounds, still tied up, were going mad trying to get after them. A number of guards had arrived and were doing their best to separate the different factions but individual battles were being waged all over the field. The large woman was laying about her in all directions, the little man encouraging her by jumping up and down and shouting in a thin, reedy voice.

"Where's Molly?" Hennessy asked, looking anxiously about him. He knew his grandmother's propensity for getting into trouble.

"There she is," Brooks pointed. "Over there by the van."

Molly was struggling with a man who appeared to be wearing a gaily-coloured hat, but when they got closer, they saw that it was the parrot, Mabel, perched on his head. The bird was furiously pecking at any part of him that came within its range.

"Atta girl," Brooks cried, "give it to him proper..."

"Get it off me," the man roared. "The bloody beast is destroying me."

Hennessy was quite enjoying the spectacle: it was

the first time that Mabel's contrary nature had come in useful. Suddenly the bird gave an almighty squawk and rose up in the air and for a moment it looked as if she had scalped her unfortunate victim. Between her claws she triumphantly bore what appeared to be a full head of hair. However in a moment it became obvious that the man had been wearing a wig, for the head that was revealed was as bald as the proverbial egg.

Before the parrot could return to the attack, the man turned and ran off and disappeared into the crowd. Molly, too, had lost her hat in the mêlée and her hair was standing on end as though an electric current had been drilled through it. The light of battle was in her eyes and it was clear that she was casting about for someone else to belabour.

"Don't you think it's time we got out of here?" Hennessy asked her. "The guards've arrived in force and it'll only be a matter of time before they begin arresting people."

Reluctantly Molly allowed herself to be led towards the gap in the fence. Just as they got there one of the original custodians appeared and made a grab at Molly. No sooner had he laid a hand on her than Mabel appeared, dropping out of the sky like a miniature dive bomber, claws poised, beak snapping.

"Holy Mother of God," the tough breathed, throwing his arms up to protect his head. He beat at the irate parrot. Then he too took off and fled in panic.

Hennessy helped Molly along with a hand under

her elbow, and they made their way back down the lane. With every step Molly protested that she wanted to stay there and be arrested: "I'm ready to go to prison for my beliefs," she cried. "No use saying one thing and doing the other. I want my day in court…"

"If they find out you're the owner of that man-eating parrot they'll put you in for 999 years," Hennessy told her. "Let's get out of here while the going's good."

Back at the cars the protesters were beginning to regroup. The large woman and the small man were there, both plainly satisfied by the day's work. "I'm proud of you all," the woman told them. "We succeeded in disrupting the meeting, we released the hares and we gave those bloodthirsty coursing people something to think about. We've won the battle, but the war is not over. Keep the faith, comrades, and ultimate victory will be ours."

A cheer went up and a couple of the men attempted to hoist the woman up on to their shoulders, but they soon desisted when they found how heavy she was. Everyone was smiling and slapping one another on the back, warriors who had triumphed in a just cause.

They were so busy congratulating each other that they failed to notice the strange looking vehicle that was backing up the lane towards them. It was a large, cylindrical container on four wheels and it was being propelled by a reversing tractor.

The clanking and banging it was making finally broke in on them and they began turning in its direction. It came up to just short of the last parked car and stopped. A grim-looking man in a flat cap and torn anorak got down from the tractor and came around to the rear of the container.

Taking his time he unhooked a metallic hose with a wide nozzle, fiddled with a number of levers and then turned to face the assembled protesters.

"What are you doing, my man?" the large woman asked him in a bossy tone.

"Well, seeing as you're all full of it, you'll recognise what this is soon enough," the man confronting her said.

He hoisted up the hose, turned one final lever and immediately a stream of evil-smelling pig slurry whooshed out in a wide arc and descended on the victorious warriors. The effect was startling: people who but a moment before had been laughing and talking and full of good cheer now turned into a crazed rabble. Slithering and sliding, they fell back in the face of the torrent of foulness that was battering them. In their haste to get away they knocked one another over, rolled on the ground, crawled on their hands and knees. The large woman, a little way back, began to shout, "Get into the cars..." but, too late, found that it was a mistake to have opened her mouth.

Hennessy had been one of the first to recognise what the man was about and, by keeping close to the ground, he had managed to avoid the worst of the onslaught. Now he wrenched open the door of the Volkswagen and threw himself inside, but he was too late to avoid being accompanied by a slash of the slurry. The stench was sick-making in the confines of the car and in the grip of it he felt his stomach heave.

Later that evening it was an ill-looking and ill-feeling threesome that made its way back to Dublin. No words could properly express their feelings, so they rode along in silence.

Only the parrot seemed unfazed by the catastrophe. Possibly it lacked a sense of smell or maybe the aroma of pig-dirt was part of its natural habitat. Seemingly unaffected either way it talked and whistled all the way home.

9

On the Monday Hennessy asked Brooks what his parents had thought of his condition when he arrived home. Molly had simply dropped him outside his house and then taken off, discretion being the better part of valour.

"My mother burned all my clothes," Brooks said ruefully. "I was confined to barracks for the rest of the weekend. I think she's writing to your grandmother…"

"What'd your father say?"

"I don't have a father."

"Oh?"

"He's gone."

"Dead?"

"No, just departed."

It was break time and they were standing in a corner out of the wind. Both Swift and O'Brien were absent without leave: someone said they'd been seen earlier in the day scuttling in the direction of town.

"I'd like to do that some time," Brooks said wistfully.

"What?"

"Go mitching."

"Why don't you?"

"I haven't got the guts."

Hennessy looked at him critically. "You look to me as if you've plenty of guts. Too many. Why are you so fat anyway?"

Brooks blushed. He mumbled something.

"What?"

"Trouble with my glands," he said again more loudly. He looked around to see if anyone else was listening. "I only have to look at something sweet and I swell up. Could be anxiety either, the doctor says, but he's told me I'll grow out of it."

"You'd better or you'll explode."

"You think it's funny, do you? Being called Puddener, and Fatso, and Man Mountain? I'm very conscious of my size and I don't need you to stand there making remarks about it."

"Take it easy. You shouldn't be so self-conscious. Anyway, it's what's inside that matters..."

"You think so?"

"Of course. I'll bet there's a thin little guy inside you right this minute struggling to get out."

"Ah, get stuffed."

"No, wait a minute." Hennessy stood in Brooks's way to prevent him from going. "What about this morning when we were doing Julius Caesar? That must have made you feel good. You know, when Caesar says, 'Let me have men about me that are fat...'?"

"Oh yeah," Brooks said furiously, "and everyone turned and looked at me and sniggered."

He caught Hennessy putting his hand in front of

his face to hide his own grin and went on, "You see? You're at it too. You're as bad as the rest of them. And to think I called you friend..."

"Aw, don't be doing the martyr."

"Then why are you laughing at me?"

"I'm not."

"Yes, you are. Look at you, you're smirking."

"That's because my face is made like that. I'm a happy fellow."

Two girls went by, arm in arm. They were wearing perfume and the scent of it sweetened the air. Hennessy sniffed appreciatively.

"Hey, Brooksie," he said, "what d'you think of the girls in this school?"

"I don't think about them."

"Come on, don't sulk. Tell me what you think."

"They're all scrogs."

"What d'you mean by that?"

"I don't know. I heard Swifty say it. Anyway, if the fellows are bad for making fun of me, the girls are worse. Could we just change the subject?"

Hennessy shrugged. He had just seen the red-haired girl who'd made the rude sign at him through the Principal's window on his first day in the school. She was in the company of a hulk dressed all in black leather that Hennessy presumed was Mad Max Bacon. Swift hadn't exaggerated about him: he was as broad as a barn door and looked as if he could go through one without waiting to open it. He had a square head, cropped hair and little ears but at this distance his crossed eyes were not noticeable.

The two of them appeared to be arguing and, as Hennessy watched, the girl suddenly flounced away and moved in their direction. Mad Max scowled after her. Then he walked around the corner and out of sight.

Surprising himself, as the girl came abreast of him, Hennessy said, "How's it going?"

She paused and made a show of looking all around her. "I think I'm hearing voices," she said. She glanced at Hennessy. "Were you addressing me by any chance?"

"You're Liz Finn, aren't you?"

"I might be. Then again I might be the Queen of Sheba. What's it to you?"

"I just wanted to say hello. I'm new here. My name's Michael Hennessy."

"I don't care if it's Jumping Jack Flash. What do I do? Genuflect? Are you a bramble stamper or what? Do I get a whiff of the great outdoors?"

Hennessy gulped, wondering for a second if he still smelled of pig slurry. He had taken so many showers over the weekend that at the end of it he felt waterlogged.

"I remember you from my first day here," he went on hurriedly. "Then later on someone told me your name."

"Was it balloon-head here?"

They both looked at Brooks, who appeared to be trying to climb into the cement wall beside him.

"No, it was someone else."

"Now, who could that have been, I wonder?

Which of my many admirers?"

"It was a guy called Swift. He's in my form. You probably know him. He's got blond hair and spots..."

"Spots? Ugh..." The girl shuddered. Up close her skin was stark white but her eyes were outlined in purple eye shadow and she was wearing lipstick of the same colour. Her red hair still had the orange streak at one side.

"He plays the drums," Hennessy said, feeling that he'd let Swift down by saying he had spots.

"A spotty drummer," the girl said. She wrinkled her nose. "You keep funny company, buster. Funny as in "ha ha" funny. Michelin Man here and a spotty drummer, yet..." She laughed and began moving away as the bell to end break time rang. "Maybe we'll trade the verbals again," she said over her shoulder. "That's me, I'll do anything for a laugh."

Hennessy watched her go, his mouth open. He was thinking that he'd never met anyone quite like her before in his life.

That evening, as his bus moved through the city centre, Hennessy saw Swift and O'Brien walking along O'Connell Street. He got off at the next stop and caught up with them.

O'Brien was carrying a plastic bag that clanked by his side with each step he took. "What've you got there?" Hennessy asked, and was surprised when O'Brien looked at him warningly and shook his head.

"They're cassettes," Swift said, putting his mouth

up close to Hennessy's ear. "He nicked them."

"You mean he stole them?"

"Will you keep your voice down…You don't need to tell the whole world, do you?"

Hennessy gazed at O'Brien's open and seemingly honest face. He had freckles and a mop of brown hair. It wasn't the appearance of someone who went about nicking things.

"That's the beauty of it," Swift said, after they had gone into a Kylemore cafe and were sitting eating buns and drinking coffee, "no one ever suspects him of being a tea-leaf—"

"Tea-leaf?"

"—thief. Now if it was me…I look like a crook."

"That's true."

"Hi, no need to be so quick to agree with me."

"No, it's just that I see what you mean. O'Brien looks like someone you'd trust with your last pound…"

"I wouldn't trust him with my first one."

Hennessy was still shocked at the idea of the two of them spending the day in town stealing cassettes. "Would you not be afraid of getting caught?" he asked. "Think of what your parents'd say…"

Swift choked on a mouthful of coffee. He put down the mug and wiped his mouth. "That's exactly what happened to O'Brien's old man," he said. "He got caught. Now he's up in the 'Joy on his holidays."

"Your father's in gaol?"

"Well, he's not on the Riviera…"

"What did he rob?"

Swift grinned: "A labour exchange..."

Hennessy was finding it difficult to come to terms with what he was being told. "Was it in the Cause?" he asked.

"The Cause?"

"You know...The lads...The Republican Cause..."

"Oh, it was in a cause alright." Swift looked at O'Brien, who winked back at him. "It was in the cause of keeping him in beer and cigarette money. Charity begins at home in O'Brien's family."

Hennessy sat back and tried to digest what he had been told. This was outside his experience. He thought of his own father and wondered if he'd treat it as lightly if he'd been put in gaol for robbing a labour exchange. "Why a labour exchange?" he asked, frowning.

"He was too proud to sign on," Swift said, giving a snort of laughter.

"Aw, come on, you're pulling my leg."

"No, honest to God," O'Brien said, his face serious. "I go up to visit him every Thursday. He got two years..."

"That's terrible."

"The terrible part is that he got caught," Swift said. "It's all right for you, your old man's probably got a good job. I'll bet you live in a big house, pay cash for everything you buy. Most likely get a weekly allowance..."

"That's true," Hennessy admitted.

"You see...?"

"But even if I didn't I wouldn't go around robbing

things."

"Why not?"

"Because it's...well, because it's wrong."

"What's wrong with people who have nothing taking from people who have too much?"

"Because you can't take someone else's property."

"There's plenty of guys did it and they were looked up to as heroes."

"Who, for instance?"

"Well..." Swift cast about for likely contenders: "There was Zorro...and the Cisco Kid...and the Scarlet Pimple..."

"Pimpernel."

"And what about Robin Hood? He robbed the rich to give to the poor, didn't he?"

Hennessy laughed. "None of those guys ever existed."

"Just the same," Swift said stubbornly, "some people have too much, and the rest have nothing. Doesn't seem fair to me."

"That's the way the cookie crumbles," Hennessy said. "There'll always be the haves and the have-nots..."

"Lookit that guy Branson," Swift said, warming to his theme. "He's got so much money he can spend half his life swanning around the world in a balloon. That'd be a bit of all right..."

"Is that what you'd like to do, travel around in a balloon?"

"I wouldn't mind. I'll bet he pulls birds by the barrowload..."

"Is that honest injun, Swifty?" O'Brien broke in. "Does he really lam it around in a balloon?"

"Course he does. He's got nothing else to do. He's got so much of the readies that he could buy up Ireland and still have enough left over to hire Bono to sing to him in his bath."

O'Brien whistled, obviously impressed.

"So what's a few cassettes here or there robbed from fellows like that?" Swift went on. "He'll never miss them."

"But what if everyone who goes into his stores robs a few?" Hennessy asked. "That'd soon turn him into a bankrupt."

"Ah, but there's enough like you around not to do that. You march in and plop your money down, while the likes of O'Brien and myself are skulking about trying to lift a few. In a way, I suppose, we depend on each other, you to keep guys like that solvent, us to maintain demand for what they have to sell."

Hennessy laughed. "That's a funny way to look at it."

Swift shrugged. "That's what it comes down to in the end, isn't it?" he said. "You look at it the way you have to…as the actress said to the bishop…"

They had finished their coffee, so they got up and went their separate ways. When Hennessy got home he found a brand new cassette of UB 40 in his schoolbag.

10

By the end of his second week in St Jude's, Hennessy had sussed out the scene pretty well.

Lawless, the form teacher, was tough but fair and he had a dry sense of humour. He knew how to push just hard enough to get what he wanted, but not to create a situation that he couldn't handle.

There was an easy atmosphere in his classes and, where his subject, mathematics, was concerned, he never pretended to be a know-all. He often made mistakes, calling them his deliberate errors but the class wasn't fooled. It was obvious that he did very little preparation and his method of correcting homework, as he was forever telling them, was to throw the copybooks down the stairs and those that landed face up passed, while those that landed face down failed.

The English teacher was a woman, young, athletic and tough. She had better discipline than most of the male staff; her students respected her and she had a reputation, well deserved, it appeared, for getting excellent examination results. It was also a known fact that Mr House had a crush on her but was so shy in her presence that he became dumbstruck, bothered and bewildered.

History and geography were taught by the same guy, a black-bearded barbarian who loved to dwell on the bloodier episodes on the course and who had a line in sarcasm that would burn paint off a wall. He was known as Vlad the Impaler.

Irish was a fresh-faced young guy from the West of Ireland, who had trouble with his "esses"; Commerce was a tall, thin character that you could nearly read a magazine through; French was a Corkonian with a high, fluting voice; and science was big and blond and was rumoured to use formaldehyde as a deodorant.

The class favourite, however, was the Christian Doctrine teacher: a small, oldish man with a face like a prune. Mr Badham was his name, and he was forever in a state of gentle drunkenness. At intervals during the lesson he would retire behind the portable blackboard to imbibe a little more of his "medicine" and would then return refreshed, weaving slightly and with a contented smile on his seamed face.

The Principal, Mr House, worked hard at being invisible. Marks were allotted to anyone who claimed to have seen him during the day. He was continually attending meetings outside the school, and if he was glimpsed all that was seen of him was his back and his battered briefcase as he scurried out the door.

As April droned on, all the talk in the school was about the show that was to be put on in the last weeks of term. A number of senior students had written it in collaboration with the music teacher. It was to be a rock extravaganza loosely based on the Shakespearean play *The Merchant of Venice*.

All of the main roles had been cast, but a number of hangers-on and camp-followers were needed and Hennessy and Brooks were eager to be included, Hennessy because he'd heard that Liz Finn was in it and Brooks because he believed that an appearance on the stage would do wonders for his image.

Swift and O'Brien had been roped in as members of the orchestra and, as their first gig was also coming up, they were rehearsing like mad. The two other members of the group were Tony O'Moore on bass guitar and Sean Guildea on synthesiser. O'Moore was regarded as being good but Guildea won his place purely because of the fact that he owned the synthesiser.

On a wet Wednesday when games had been scrapped, the hopefuls who were to audition for the show congregated in the school hall. Mr King, the music teacher, an excitable little man with a bald head, sat down in the body of the hall and the giggling aspirants to possible fame and fortune came out on the stage one by one to perform their various bits and pieces.

Hennessy could hold a song pretty well and had no fears but Brooks was in a terrible state and was sweating like a rain shower.

"Don't worry," Hennessy advised him, "you'll be all right. Sing out as loud as you can and whatever you do, don't stop."

"What happens if I forget the words?"

"Just go dooby dooby doo. And smile. All the best troupers keep smiling through…"

"Oh God," Brooks groaned, looking as if he were about to step onto a gallows rather than a stage.

The line shuffled along through an Elvis impersonation, a girl who sang a verse of "Ave Maria", and a guy whose voice broke right in the middle of his song. The fellow in front of Hennessy was being very brave, cracking jokes and making light of it all, but, when his number was called, he suddenly turned tail and disappeared out the door.

Hennessy sang a few lines of the Elton John number "Goodbye Norma Jean" and was quickly told that he was okay and to give his name to his class representative.

He trudged down to the back and then turned to wait for Brooks.

There was a long pause, then the man himself appeared, for all the world like a mourner at a wake. He staggered to the front of the stage, stuck out his chest, threw wide his arms and opened his mouth. Nothing came out. He gave a sickly grin, then tried again.

This time he managed a high squeak, such as a mouse with its tail caught in a trap might make. He coughed, beat his chest with the flat of his hand, cleared his throat. Still nothing. The last shreds of his confidence visibly deserting him, he began to retreat, his face still mirroring a ghastly grin.

Feeling that he had to do something, Hennessy stepped forward and shouted, "Come on, Brooksie, give it a lash. What've you got to lose?"

As though arrested in mid-flight by the hand of God, Brooks suddenly stopped going backwards and trundled towards the front of the stage again. In a surprisingly loud and resonant voice he broke into:

> *Does your chewing gum lose its flavour on the bedpost overnight?*
> *When your mother says don't chew it, do you swallow it in fright?*

Before he could get any further, Mr King held up his hand and told him to desist: "It's obvious you want to be in the show, otherwise you wouldn't have subjected yourself, and more importantly me, to such torture," he told him. "There're a number of non-singing roles, so put yourself down for one of them. And get out of here before one of us has a seizure."

Later, in Nixers, they celebrated with Coca-Cola and Mars bars. As usual the place was crowded and Bad Bob was stumping around, looking his usual unpleasant self.

"Only for you I'd never have made it," Brooks told Hennessy for the umpteenth time. He was embarrassingly grateful and kept wanting to buy him things: "Have another Mars bar," he urged. "A Kit Kat? A Crunchie? A Star Bar?"

"I've enough," Hennessy said, shaking him off. Liz Finn and two of her cronies were at a table near them and he didn't want them to see how Brooks was pulling and dragging at him.

She caught his eye and winked, and he felt a flush start at the roots of his own red hair and bleed quickly downwards.

"Excuse me a minute," he told Brooks and pushed his way over to their table.

The girl pretended she didn't see him standing at her elbow and continued talking to her girlfriends. Then, with an elaborate show, she glanced in his direction, raised her eyebrows and said, "So..?"

Somebody pushed him from behind and he almost fell in on top of her. The other two girls started giggling. He knew them slightly; one of them was called Jacinta, the other he couldn't put a name to but had seen around a lot in Liz's company. They both had back-combed hair that hid most of their faces, pale make-up, and the one whose name he didn't know had a stud in the side of her nose.

"I got a part in the play," he said, trying not to look too pleased.

"That's nice for you," Liz said. "Is it as the pound of flesh?"

"Huh?"

"I thought you might be doing the pound of flesh that Shylock wins from Antonio..."

Hennessy's face mirrored his puzzlement.

Suddenly it dawned on Liz that he hadn't read the play. "You don't know anything about it, do you?" she said.

"Not really..."

"You're a bit of a spudhead, aren't you?" The girl looked at her two companions, who laughed dutifully. "Let me set you wise," she went on. "There's this rich geezer, a Jew called Shylock, who loans a merchant, Antonio, money, on condition that, if he can't pay it back by a certain date, Shylock'll be allowed to cut a pound of flesh from Antonio's bod. You get the picture?"

"Yes," Hennessy said, sounding grateful. "So what happens?"

"Yeah, go on, Liz," chorused the two girls, "tell us what happens."

Clearly enjoying being the centre of attention, Liz continued, "Well, Antonio misses the boat and can't cough up the moola, so he's due to bare his chest and grit his teeth. But along comes this classy chick, Portia, who knows a thing or two about this and that and who has been hankering after Antonio's bod herself. She dresses up as a judge and spins Shylock a few hairy tales until his head's in a diz. In the end she gets Antonio off, but he owes her one. The Jew goes off muttering into his beard. And that's about it..."

"But guess who's playing Portia?" the girl with the stud in her nose said.

The three of them stared at Liz, who scowled and said, "Yeah, it's that bint from 5a, Mercedes McGurk. Real hoity-toity she is, with her nose stuck so far up in the air there's icicles on it. And she's got a voice like a cat in heat..."

"No, she hasn't," contradicted the girl with the

stud. "She's took singing lessons. I heard Kinger say she sings like a angel..."

Liz gave her a look that would have withered an oak tree. "Nice friend you are," she said. "You're only a wagon..."

"Liz was in for the part herself, you see," the girl explained to Hennessy. "Now she's just jealous."

"Aw, go soak your head," Liz shouted at her furiously. "Preferably in the toilet."

She stood up, almost knocking the table over. "I'm gettin' outa here before I do something I'm sorry for," she said grimly. "Youse two give me a pain where I sit down." She moved away, then, as a parting shot she told them: "Why don't you go out in a field somewhere and eat grass like the cows you are ..?"

11

Hennessy followed Liz Finn out the door of Nixers. The evening traffic was rumbling by and the buses had their interior lights on, showing the faces of people eager to be home and sitting down to their tea.

Liz went down the road, then stopped and put her back against the wall of the local picture house. She took out a cigarette but had difficulty lighting it in the wind that had sprung up. She looked mad enough to eat nails.

"Those bees," she said, "they love to get one in on you. They're back there now laughing at me."

Hennessy leaned against the wall beside her, placing his bag at his feet. He cast about in his mind for some words of consolation, and finally came up with: "You'd've been great in the part of Portia. I can just see you telling that old guy...What was his name?—"

"Shylock."

"—Yeah, Shylock, where to get off."

"Let's pass on that one, okay?"

Liz looked down at the bag at her feet, then gave it a hefty kick. There was a dull, clunking sound as the bag was propelled out into the centre of the path.

"What was in it?" she asked idly, not really interested.

Hennessy grimaced. "Well, it's my flask, actually. But don't worry, I've got another one."

There was silence, both of them busy with their own thoughts, until finally Hennessy spoke.

"What part have you in the play anyway?"

The girl moodily puffed at her cigarette and then impatiently flicked it out into the middle of the road.

"I play the part of Shylock's daughter, Jessica. She goes mooching around all the time with her nose stuck in her bib. Demure, Kinger called her. Can you imagine it? Me demure..?"

Hennessy couldn't but he didn't say so. It was as well to tread carefully with the girl in the mood she was in. He was delighted when two of his classmates from 4c passed by and glanced curiously at the pair of them. "How's it going?" he greeted them, and they nodded and grinned in reply.

Feeling that he'd better say something to the girl, he asked her, "So what d'you do? You get a bus or what?"

The girl hunched her shoulders into her jacket. "Nah," she said. "I'm expecting a lift. You go if you're in a hurry."

"Oh, I'm not in a hurry," Hennessy said hurriedly, although he knew his grandparents would be wondering where he was. Also, he had just seen his bus pass by and knew there wouldn't be another one along for at least twenty minutes.

"What d'you think of this kip?" Liz asked him,

nodding in the direction of St Jude's. She examined her fingers before beginning delicately to chew on a nail.

"I think it's great," Hennessy answered enthusiastically. "I was in another place as a boarder but it didn't hold a candle to St Jude's."

"A boarder, eh? You must be a bit of a nob..."

Hennessy told her about his parents being in Africa, and how he'd also spent most of his life out there. That awakened more than a slight interest in the girl, so much so that she left off biting her nails.

"What's it like out in Africa?" she asked. "Pretty hot, is it? Lots of snakes and stuff..?"

He started telling her what Africa was like but she interrupted him in the middle of it to inform him that she was going to be a hairdresser: "I've been promised a place in town when I finish my course. In Drago's. Have you heard of it? Twink goes there to have her hair done."

"Is that right?" Hennessy said, a little put out because of the girl's lack of interest in his account of Africa.

"It's unisex. You could go there if you wanted."

Hennessy had a mental picture of Christy the barber who had his shop up on the North Circular and gave him a short back and sides once a month for one pound fifty. He tried to imagine Twink sitting in the chair among all the old age pensioners. The mind boggled...

"I could probably get you a discount," the girl told him loftily. "I'm well in there. I do four hours every

Saturday morning."

Hennessy had lost the thread of the conversation. "Where's that again?" he asked.

"In Drago's. Are you listening to what I'm saying or is that just the wind whistling between your ears?"

"Sorry, sorry...Where did you say that place is...Drago's?"

"Centre city, off Grafton Street. But I'm not sure if it'd really suit you. Pretty chintzy people go in there..."

"Thanks very much..."

But Liz had ceased leaning against the wall and was moving towards the edge of the path. "Here's my lift," she said. "I've gotta go. Catch you later, alligator."

A large, powerful-looking motor bike had drawn up to the kerb, the figure astride it parcelled up in familiar-looking black leather. As Hennessy watched, the smoked glass visor of the helmet was pushed up and a pair of remarkable looking Ben Turpin eyes were revealed. They both glared—at him, he presumed, but he wasn't exactly sure as they were looking in different directions at the same time.

It needed no great brainpower on his part to recognise the fact the he was in the presence of Mad Max Bacon, the terror of the town. He had only seen him in the distance up to this; up close the experience reminded him of the time he'd seen his first rhinoceros.

Liz swung herself up onto the pillion, while Bacon continued his red-eyed glare. "Nice bike," Hennessy said, being sociable.

"What's it to you, looper?" Bacon growled, his voice magnified by the echo chamber of his helmet. He revved up the engine and the back wheel made smoke.

"Just making a comment. Being friendly, like."

"Who asked you to stick your garden hose into my business?"

"Garden hose?"

"Nose," Liz supplied.

"Nobody. Pardon me for living..."

"You won't be if I find you messing with my mot again."

"I was just passing the time of day. Until you came along to carry her off on your Ben Hur."

"Huh?"

"Chariot."

What Hennessy guessed was a frown distorted further Bacon's features. He opened the throttle and after an initial roar the engine abruptly cut out. Dismayed, Hennessy hurriedly stepped back.

"Take it easy," Liz said soothingly to her hero. "I'm in a hurry. Let it go..."

Bacon raised a huge Doc-Martined foot and gave the bike an almighty kick start and, to Hennessy's relief, it spluttered into life. The visor was lowered, the shoulders tensed but, instead of moving off into the line of traffic, Bacon forced the front wheel up over the kerb.

Hennessy snatched up his bag and took off, the noise of the motor bike exploding the evening air behind him. Other pedestrians had to scatter as the

huge machine thundered along the path and it was
only when Hennessy dodged into a shop doorway
that Bacon swung back onto the road. The two of
them disappeared into the snarl of traffic but a large
cloud of blue smoke remained to bear witness to Mad
Max's threatening presence.

As both Molly and Pop were out that night, Hennessy
had invited O'Brien and his group up to practise.
They set up their equipment in the dining room and
for an hour-and-a-half the walls of the ancient house
pulsed to a racket that probably made even the
ghosts think they were being haunted.

Hennessy stood it for a while, then he went up to
his room, plugged in his earphones and listened to
the reggae sounds of UB 40. They were like a heavenly
choir compared to the devil music below.

When eventually the noise had subsided to the
odd rat-a-tat-tat on the drums, he went down and
joined them. The four of them looked as if they'd run
the Dublin marathon. O'Brien was lying on the
ground, Guildea and O'Moore had the blank eyed
stare of zombies and Swift was sitting among his
drum kit like someone who wasn't too sure if he'd
survived an earthquake or not.

"Had a successful session?" Hennessy asked.

"Wha?"

Swift shook his head and pointed to his ears, and
Hennessy realised that they were all suffering from
temporary deafness. He went out to the kitchen and
brought in coke and crisps and shared them out. The

silence in the room still seemed to buzz with the noise they had been making.

When they had got their hearing back, Hennessy told them about his encounter with Mad Max: "He drove the bike up onto the path and tried to run me down. He must be some kind of maniac..."

"I told you," Swift said. "He's a grade A nutter."

"But how can he afford to have a bike like that?"

"He's loaded. His Da is into market gardening out somewhere near Skerries. Max helps him. I think he shovels the...ah, pig slurry?"

"Oh God," Hennessy groaned, blessing himself, "Not that. Don't mention the pig slurry..."

"Sorry. But there's a lot of money in it. I've read somewhere that you can even make perfume out of it. Just dab a little pig slurry perfume behind your ears and the girls'll climb all over you..."

Swift did a drum roll, then flipped both sticks in the air and caught them on the way down. "Someone should do something about Bacon," he said. "He gets away with murder. Some of the teachers even are afraid of him."

"Be my guest," O'Moore said. "I'm not going to have anything to do with him. He wrestles bulls every morning before he comes into school."

"Get out've it," O'Brien said.

"It's true. Markie O'Keefe told me and he comes in that way every day."

"Holy jumpin' Jerusalem!"

"It'd have to be a case of mind over matter," Hennessy said, thinking aloud. "Brains over brawn."

"That's it," Swift agreed. He winked at Hennessy. "You want to put him in the way of a fall, don't you Henno? Got an ulterior motive, as they say..."

The four of them looked at him and he said, "What does she see in him anyway? He's like King Kong..."

Guildea worked the synthesiser and coaxed an ape-like roar out of it. It was answered by a squawk from the next room.

"What's that?" O'Brien asked, looking jumpy.

"Just Mabel the parrot," Hennessy told him. "She might be able for Bacon if she got a good run at him. She's wicked enough..."

Swift stretched, then began to pack up his drum kit. It fitted into two coffin-like boxes with rope handles. "Well Saturday night is the big night," he said. "Our first professional engagement..."

"And maybe our last," O'Moore said gloomily.

"Aw, cut that out," O'Brien told him hotly. "We have to start somewhere. The Beatles began in a hole in the ground."

"That's where we could end up too, only buried."

"Are you coming down to see us?" Swift asked Hennessy. "You haven't been to the Bower as yet."

"I'm not much good at dancing."

"Dancing!" Swift rolled his eyes to the heavens. "There's not room to move, never mind dance. If someone fainted in there he wouldn't fall down until everyone had gone home. It's just one solid, heaving mass..."

"I'll think about it," Hennessy said. "I really

should do some studying. The Inter's only a month away."

The others hooted, and Guildea blew a raspberry on the synthesiser.

12

Hennessy stood in front of the mirror and gazed unhappily at his reflection. He had brushed half a tub of Brylcreem into his hair and still it wouldn't sit down. He tried creasing it up the middle but the two wings that resulted made him look as if he had a miniature ski slope on his head. He was also developing a pimple on the end of his nose.

"Typical," he muttered, scowling at himself.

He left his room and tiptoed into his grandparent's bedroom. Eyeing the assortment of jars and bottles on the dressing table, he selected one that looked promising and took it back to his own room.

It was a plastic tube with "Fresh Look Make-Up" printed on the side.

He unscrewed the cap and sniffed. It had no scent. Tentatively he eased a little of the milk chocolate coloured goo out on to his finger.

He glanced around to make sure he wasn't observed; then he spread it carefully over the swelling redness on his nose. He rubbed it well in, manfully bearing the pain. When he was finished the make-up appeared to have gone and the pimple with it.

Satisfied, he returned the tube. He hesitated over a jar of hair gel but decided that if it didn't work he'd have to wash his hair all over again and he couldn't face the prospect of that.

He was wearing stone-washed jeans and a black silk shirt that Molly had given him for Christmas. His runners were in the washing machine in the kitchen. He had used Pop's electric razor to remove the down from his face, slapped after-shave on his cheeks, squirted deodorant under his arms and cleaned under his fingernails with his penknife. His Wrangler jacket was laid·out on the bed…

"Cripes," he told his reflection, "I'm done up like a dog's dinner and I smell like a bunch of sweet violets…Am I nuts or what?"

He sat down on the bed and crossed his legs. Then he re-crossed them, left over right. He put his elbow on his knee, his chin on his hand. He began to whistle.

Straightening up, he said out loud, "I don't know what I'm so nervous about. It's only an old dance. I'll go down there and I'll only be a face in the crowd. I won't have to make conversation with anyone because the music'll be too loud to hear an ass hee-haw…"

He got up and checked himself out again. He wished he was about six inches taller, broader in the chest and had long blond hair. He tried sneering, but decided it made him look as if he had just got wind of a bad smell.

He put on the jacket, went downstairs and got his runners from the washing machine. The laces were missing and he was searching for them when his grandmother came in, the parrot perched as usual on her shoulder.

"Going out then, are we?"

Hennessy paused in his search, the drawer of the kitchen table gaping open. It was filled to overflowing with all kinds of junk: tubes of glue and paint, balls of twine, mothballs, coloured spools of thread, a roll of insulating tape...But no shoelaces.

"You can never find anything around here," he complained bitterly. He rummaged around again and then cried out in pain. When he took his hand out of the drawer it was to show Molly the mousetrap that had imprisoned two of his fingers.

"Serves you right for being so impatient," Molly said unsympathetically. "What're you looking for anyway?"

"Laces," Hennessy said, gingerly prising the trap off his hand.

Molly leaned up to a shelf over the cooker and came down with the red-tipped strings.

"You hid them up there," Hennessy said accusingly.

"No," she corrected him, "I put them up there for safety. Remember how Mabel ate the last lot."

Hennessy did up his shoes while Molly washed her hands in white spirit at the sink. The pungent smell filled the kitchen.

"So, what do you think?" Hennessy asked her. "How do I look?"

"I thought you said you'd never wear that shirt."

"Why, what's wrong with it?"

"Nothing, it looks great on you. But when I gave it to you, you made little of my taste."

"It's come back into fashion since then. Black silk is all the rage."

"It should be. It cost enough."

"You told me you got it second-hand."

"Did I?"

"That's what you said…"

The parrot, growing tired of listening to the conversation, spread her wings and flew up to the trapeze-like perch that had been rigged up for her and hung from the ceiling. A feather floated in the air and settled gently on the open butter-dish.

Wrinkling his nose with distaste, Hennessy said, "That bird is coming apart. She's disgusting…"

"She's moulting. It's that time of year."

Molly dried her hands, then sighed and sat down on a wooden kitchen chair. She looked tired.

"Why don't I make a cup of tea for you?" Hennessy offered. "You look as if you could do with one."

"I'd rather have a gin and tonic."

He made one for her, dumping in a slice of lemon and loads of ice. Behind her back he took a swig from the gin bottle. It tasted like the white spirit she'd washed her hands in.

"So, this dance you're going to, is it being held in the school?"

"No, it's in a place called the Bower, which is attached to another school. But it's run by teachers. I'm only going to hear the 4-Ups…"

"The 4 whats?"

"Swift and O'Brien and two other fellows. You met them the other night."

"What kind of music do they play?"

"A sort of rock and roll."

"Rock and roll? I thought that'd gone out of fashion years ago?"

"It's come back in again—like the silk shirt."

"How are you for money?"

"I'm okay."

"Well...enjoy yourself."

"It's the first dance I've ever been to..."

"There always has to be a first time..."

"Yeah, I guess so."

As he was turning to go, Molly said. "Michael, I'm glad you like your new school, and that you've made some new friends. We're not a very emotional lot in our family but you must know that Caskey and I love you very much. We're delighted you've settled down..."

"I know that," Hennessy said, not meeting her eye. He couldn't think of anything more to say.

Not so the parrot, however. Giving a rude squawk, she proclaimed in her sing-song voice: "Get up the yard, get up the yard, Henno is a poofter."

13

"I'm going to kill that bloody bird," Hennessy told Brooks when they met at the appointed place a little after eight o'clock. "I'll poison her, then shoot her, then drown her…"

"That's what they did to Rasputin."

"Who?"

"A Russian priest who advised the Czar before the revolution."

"What'd he advise him?"

"To get rid of the nobles and tax the peasants. Or was it the other way round?"

"I don't know, I never heard of him. Where d'you pick up that kind of stuff anyway?"

"In history class. You were there…"

"I mustn't've been listening."

They were standing at the bottom of Vernon Avenue and out across the estuary the lights of the deep-sea port were pin-pricks in the night. A cold, raw wind made them hunch their shoulders into their jackets and in the sky the stars played hide-and-seek with scraps of cloud.

"So, what'll we do?" Hennessy asked, shifting from foot to foot. "Will we go on up there?"

"May as well."

"What's the routine?"

"I'm not sure. I've only ever been to one dance and then I didn't go in."

"What d'you mean? How could you have been at a dance if you didn't go in?"

"I got cold feet at the last minute. I walked around for a couple of hours and then went home. I was afraid they'd make fun of me."

"Why? Were you wearing your underpants over your trousers or what?"

"They laugh at me all the time."

"Here we go again. Who is they? Who laughs at you all the time?"

"You know," Brooks said, "people..."

"It's only your imagination. Listen if you go in there with the idea that people will laugh at you, then they will. Have a bit of confidence. Sneer at them. Imagine you're Mickey Rourke or Rob Lowe..."

Brooks didn't seem convinced. "Some of them go for a few drinks beforehand," he said.

"Is that what you want to do?"

"I've never had a drink."

"My God, you're really something. You've never been to a dance. You've never had a drink. If you'd been in the Garden of Paradise you'd never have been thrown out. Think of all the trouble that'd've saved us."

They walked up Vernon Avenue, both of them dawdling. A group of fat and out-of-condition footballers passed by, grunting and groaning and leaving behind them a smell of sweat that could have been cut into chunks and sold as fly-repellent.

As they drew near their destination they began to encounter other groups bound in the same direction as themselves. The talk was all about identity cards and how best to smuggle in the various bottles they were furtively drinking from.

"I was caught rapid last week," a fellow named Mickey English told them. "The guy whose card I was using had been knocked down by a bus. His name was in all the papers. Lawless said to me, all sarky like, 'Glad to see you've made such a quick recovery. Some class of miracle, was it?' He gave me the bum's rush so fast I nearly passed myself by."

"So what'll you do this week?"

"I've got another sod's card, Be just my luck to find he's dropped dead of a heart attack."

They turned into a badly-lit driveway and moved round the side of a large block of buildings. Immediately they were in the midst of a pushing and shoving crowd of fellows and girls, all intent on getting through a door that was only wide enough to admit two at a time.

Hennessy lost sight of Brooks but he was too busy looking out for his own welfare to worry about him. Lucky for him he got caught up in a wave that was going forward and he went through the door with the abruptness of a cork coming out of a bottle. He was travelling so fast that, for an instant, he feared he'd be propelled right through the hall and out the back door.

The beefy arm of a large individual with a crew-cut and drooping moustache put paid to his forward progress; he had to show his card and pay the entrance fee. He was handed a pink ticket. Then he had to turn out his pockets to prove he wasn't carrying any of the forbidden alcohol. The bouncer also made him haw into his face so that he could smell his breath.

Having gone through the formalities, he was motioned in under an archway that opened on to a long corridor. The hall itself was to his right, a huge, barn-like room with a raised section at one end and curtained windows high up on the walls. At this early hour it was still only half full, the lights were on and, although a pop tune was thudding out, no one was dancing.

Hennessy went over to the drinks counter and bought himself a Coke. There were a few people about that he knew, but only to nod to, and he was relieved when he saw Brooks looming up.

When he saw how he was dressed, though, he had second thoughts on the matter. He was wearing baggy black trousers and a technicolor Hawaiian shirt, with of all things, parrots on it. Also his hair was upswept into hedgehog points, giving him the Young Einstein appearance of someone who'd struck his finger into a live electric socket and was living to regret it. For someone who was afraid he'd be laughed at, he was about as inconspicuous as a naked man in a church.

"You like the gear?" he asked Hennessy. "Pretty cool, huh?"

"You could say that, I suppose."

"Jealousy'll get you nowhere."

In time, the hall filled up. The dee-jay was a middle aged fellow called Cyril. He was as thin as a pole and his small head on a long thin neck flicked about snake-like to the beat of the music. He kept up an incessant stream of jive, of which Hennessy couldn't understand a word; then, every so often, he'd come out with slogans like "The boogie man'll get you if you don't watch out" which the dancers dutifully repeated after him.

The first hour was devoted to heavy metal and trash metal, with Black Sabbath figuring large. Fellows danced with fellows, girls with girls, in a rugby scrum that heaved and contracted to the thundering beat.

Hennessy and Brooks drifted around the edges of this. Then throwing caution to the winds, they dived in. It was rough but exhilarating. The very floor and walls seemed to reverberate, and drops of sweat flew through the air like spring showers. After a time it became a question merely of jumping up and down and the floor became a trampoline with just a slight give in it.

At ten o'clock Cyril called a halt and announced that he was going to take a break. He reassured them, however, that he had a live group for them that he was sure they were going to give a great welcome to:

"You'll know these lads," he told them, "and I think you'll agree with me that they've bags of talent. So put your hands together for...The 4-Ups!"

The curtain behind the dee-jay parted to reveal

O'Brien, Swift, O'Moore and Guildea. They were wearing identical black shirts with silver flashings and white baggies with turn-ups. There was a tremendous cheer and another even mightier one when O'Brien struck a chord and did a pelvic roll.

For the next half-hour there was pandemonium, as the band played one set after another, each one louder than the last. Those at the front crowded up around the stage and the crush was stifling. A shuttered spotlight began to revolve, and orange, crimson and purple beams flickered across open mouths, bulging eyes and waving hands. The crowd went into a state of near-hysteria, as they jumped, shouted and stamped their feet; the music was a sledgehammer striking a metal surface. On the evidence of this first gig, there was no doubt that the 4-Ups were a runaway success...

By eleven things had quietened down. Cyril was playing slow sets and guys and girls had got into some heavy smooching. The fellows with no partners congregated in the corridor and at the soft drinks counter. The trouble makers who hadn't been allowed in had drifted away. Bouncers and teachers alike were able to draw their breaths, nip around the back for a cigarette and congratulate each other on a job well done.

Hennessy's night was made too; Liz Finn had appeared and without her hulking minder.

"Where's Mad Max?" Hennessy greeted her, when he met her in the corridor. "Is he dancing in there with his motor bike?"

"He's banned," she told him, seeming surprised that he didn't know. "He's banned from every school activity, even from coming to school."

"That's a bit of all right." Summoning up courage, he went on, "Will you do me the honour of this dance?"

She squinted at him suspiciously. "Are you putting me on? The honour..."

"Well, would you like to shake a leg then?"

She'd apparently made it up with her two friends, for all three of them were together. Now she turned and winked at them. "Okay, Shorty," she said, "I'll give it a go."

Hennessy led her into the hall, then turned to face her. Now that the sought-for moment had come, he wasn't quite sure how to proceed.

Impatiently tossing her head, the girl asked him, "What's the matter? Are you paralysed or somethin'? Christmas'll be here and we won't have moved. People'll think we've put down roots."

Carefully Hennessy put his arms around her and, holding her away from him, began to move. With a snort Liz caught hold of him and pulled him close. Over her shoulder Hennessy saw other couples pasted together, dreamy-eyed, barely moving...

"That's Kylie Minogue, isn't it?" Liz said after a moment, her breath hot against his ear.

"Where?"

"Singing, you thick. Don't you know anything?"

"I know one thing."

"What?"

"It's great dancing with you."

"You're not going to go all sloppy on me, are you? That's just for the birds..."

They moved down towards the back of the hall, weaving in and out among the other dancers. One of the bouncers was standing by a double door and he had opened it slightly, obviously to let in some air. As they slowly turned, Hennessy, his mind elsewhere, noticed movement in the crack of the door. An eye was staring fixedly at him, an eye that was all too familiar; its companion would undoubtedly have been glaring at him too if it hadn't been looking off in a different direction. Hennessy felt the hair stand up on the back of his head and a shiver of fright, like ice water, ran down his spine.

"What's the matter?" the girl asked, feeling the sudden tension in him.

He opened his mouth, but no sound came out. He wet his lips and tried again? "Don't look now," he said, "but I think Mad Max has his eye on you. And on me too..."

"Where?"

"Over there—the open door..."

Liz twisted around and looked. Suddenly she grinned and it dawned on Hennessy that she wasn't very surprised. "You knew he'd be there, didn't you?" he accused her. "You wanted him to see us together. You were only playing with me..."

The girl shrugged. "We're snared rapid anyway," she said. "But who cares? The night was a real bummer. Now maybe we'll see some action. I hope you're able to run fast. Like greased lightning, for instance?"

14

It was a question, really, of life or death: Hennessy's life or death. Short of digging a tunnel, there was no way he could get out of the Bower without encountering Mad Max.

All doors except the front one were securely bolted, with a bouncer guarding each one. Everyone had to leave by the same exit: it was the rule since a couple of hard chaws had left the back door ajar, crept back in when everyone had gone home, and did unmentionable things to the hall.

He could have thrown himself on the mercy of Mr Lawless, told him the predicament he was in and asked for his protection but he knew if he did that he'd be the laughing stock of the school.

He was backstage with the 4-Ups and Brooks and it was getting to one o'clock and the end of the dance.

"The six of us could take him on," Brooks said. "He'd surely back down then."

"There's no way I'm going up against Mad Max Bacon," Guildea said. He looked around at the rest of them. "You all feel the same but you're too cowardly to say it."

"I can't expect you to put yourselves in the way of a beating for my sake," Hennessy agreed. "I'll go out and face him. He might let me off with a warning…"

"Yes, and it might snow pound notes." Swift grinned sourly. "He enjoys breaking people's bones. He's like a human JCB."

They began packing away their instruments, none of them meeting Hennessy's eye. Suddenly Brooks gave an exclamation: "Hey, wait a minute. I've got an idea. I think I know how we'll get Henno out without his being seen."

"Good old Brooksie," Swift said. "I always knew there must've been some good reason why your head is that big. I'll bet you've got a brain the size of a turnip."

"Very funny."

"No, wait a minute. Let him talk."

"Well, it's like this." Brooks paused for effect. "You see that case that Swiftie uses for his drum kit? Henno is small enough to fit into it and he's pretty light. If a couple of us carried it out with him inside..?"

Swift looked down at the case, open in front of him.

"What d'you think, Henno?"

"No way, José. That thing is like a coffin."

"Well, at least it'd only be a pretend coffin. If Maxie gets his maulers on you it'll be the real thing."

"Just get into it and try it out," Brooks urged. "That can't do any harm."

Reluctantly Hennessy stepped into the case, his face grim.

"If you scrunch down I'll be able to close the lid,"

Swift said.

He did so, bending his legs and folding his arms across his body. "How'm I going to breathe?" he asked. "I'll suffocate in here."

"It'll only be for a couple of minutes," Brooks said. "Maybe you could hold your breath..."

"Ah, this is ridiculous," Hennessy said, standing up again. "What can he do to me anyway? I'll scoot out the door like a road runner and be up the North Circular before Mad Max's second eye has a chance to spot me."

"Ah, go on, Henno, for the crack..."

Hennessy scowled. "You lot are enjoying this. You just want me to do this so that you'll have a good story to tell..."

"That's not true. We're worried about your welfare."

"Then why're you grinning?"

Swift appealed to the others, throwing his arms out wide: "Am I grinning? I ask you, am I grinning? Here I am, willing to sacrifice my drum kit to save my mate's life, and I get accused of making a skit of him. Talk about ingratitude..."

"Oh, all right," Hennessy said. He got back into the container and took up his former excruciating position.

"Who's a good boy, then?" Swift said, winking at the others. "Just bend your head a little..."

"I'm not a ruddy contortionist."

"...that's it. A little more..."

Swift clicked the lid into place, then sat on it.

From under him came a muffled groan, then silence.

"The next question is, who's going to carry it? I can't manage it on my own."

There was a studied lack of enthusiasm from his companions.

"Don't all rush to be the first. Where's your sense of decency, men? Who dares, wins..."

"I'll do it, Swifty," Brooks said. "I can't run fast anyway, so I may as well give you a hand."

"Well done, Corporal Brooks," Swift said, saluting him. "I'll see that you're mentioned in dispatches."

They hurriedly made their way down the hall, Swift and Brooks between them lugging the drum case. At the door they had a bad moment when they saw Mr Lawless staring hard at them, but he made no comment and allowed them through.

A number of fellows and girls began telling them how good the group had been, and O'Brien was inclined to dawdle. "Keep going, you mallet-head," Swift told him, pushing him along in front of him, "he's not Dracula, you know."

The first person they encountered outside was Max Bacon, looming large in his black leather and laced boots. A few of his cronies had gathered round, obviously looking forward to a bit of fun. Standing a little way apart were Liz Finn and her two friends.

The drum case was beginning to give out some ominous creaking sounds and Swift made a face at the perspiring Brooks. They pushed ahead and were almost past the group when Bacon stepped forward and put out his hand.

"Where's that squirt that pals around with you, Swift?" he growled. "The one with the lah-de-dah voice and the short back and sides…"

"Don't know who you mean, Maxie."

"Yes, you do! Hennessy."

"Oh, him. He's hiding in the jakes, I think. Knows you're after him. They'll be scouring out the joint soon, so he'll be turfed out."

"Yah."

Bacon looked suspicious but he stepped back and allowed them to proceed.

They moved more quickly along but the container was beginning to sag in the middle and the creaks were becoming splintering noises. "Holy Jumping Joseph, this thing is coming apart at the seams," Swift muttered. "Can't you go any faster?"

"I'm doing my best," Brooks protested. "It's a ton weight."

They were just about to go round the main school building when there was an almighty crack and the bottom fell out of the case, tumbling a distraught Hennessy on to the ground. Brooks fell over him, and the two of them sprawled in the gravel.

Behind them, Bacon let out a roar, pawed the ground and took off in their direction like a crazed bull.

Normally Hennessy who moved like greased lightning when he had to—and that was quite often—could easily have evaded Bacon's mad rush but this was no normal occasion. His confinement in the drum case had left him with a feeling of near panic and his abrupt release had done nothing to calm him. The final straw was having the bulky Brooks fall on top of him: that last one he could definitely have done without.

Fortunately for him, Mad Max was not exactly quick on his pins and, by the time he arrived on the scene, Hennessy was on his feet and poised for flight. He was prevented from making a clean getaway, however, when one of Bacon's large paws caught hold of the back of his jacket.

Bravely the sprawling Brooks then took a hand. He wrapped himself round Max's right leg and held on for dear life. Entangled together, the three of them presented an interesting spectacle: Hennessy, his arms flailing madly, frantically trying to depart; Bacon just as frantically holding on; and Brooks being dragged along the ground like a tortoise being wrenched out of its shell.

To highlight their struggle the headlamps of a car suddenly lit up the scene, something that gave all three of them cause to pause. The door of the vehicle opened and Mr Lawless, judge and jury combined, got out.

"What's all this, then?" he asked, sounding curious rather than angry. "Some new kind of dance?" He stood and surveyed the tableau in front of him, then he said, mock critically, "Take it from me: it'll never catch on."

The rest of the onlookers had gathered round to see the fun, their faces lit starkly by the beams from the car. No one spoke as they waited with bated breath.

"Have you all been struck dumb or what?" Lawless asked. "I've told you before that this kind of horseplay is out. It gives these dances a bad name. Have you no homes to go to?"

His intervention had broken the spell, and the three chief actors in the drama sheepishly let go of one another. Hennessy shrugged his jacket back on to his shoulders; Bacon scowled and muttered under his breath; Brooks stood up and dusted himself down. The tension subsided as palpably as a punctured tyre.

"Now, on yer bikes," Lawless ordered, his voice still mild and conversational. "I'll be following on behind and if there's any more commotion I'll be dug out of the lot of you. The three ballet dancers can stay behind. I want a word with you."

The rest of them began shuffling off, while Hennessy, Brooks and Bacon remained.

Lawless waited until everyone was out of earshot before he spoke, then he said, "Let's see now…First of all you Bacon, you great ox, you shouldn't be around here at all. You've been banned from these dances for an indefinite period—which means forever. You're never out of trouble. Your poor father has a path worn to the school coming down to bail you out. You should be ashamed of yourself. Are you ashamed of yourself?"

Bacon glared murderously at Lawless, his hands clenching and unclenching by his sides. Finally, between gritted teeth, he growled, "Yeah."

"Yeah? You mean yes?"

"Yes."

"Yes what?"

"Yes, sir."

"That's better. Now, go and get that infernal machine of yours and wheel it out the gate before you start it up. It makes enough noise to wake the dead."

Bacon slouched off and in a moment reappeared pushing his motor bike. As he passed Brooks and Hennessy he gave them a look that could have started a forest fire. Plainly he was implying that the path of true friendship between them was still littered with many obstacles.

When he had disappeared from sight, Lawless said, "You two should have more sense than to become involved with the likes of him." He held up his hand as Brooks attempted to speak: "I don't want to hear anything about it. It's late, it's past my bedtime and I've a headache from that noise that you laughingly call music. Just thank your lucky stars that I came along, otherwise you'd be dog's meat. On your way..."

After a couple of heartfelt "thank you sir's, they both made their way down the drive and on to the road. Cautiously they peered up and down it, but there was no sign of Mad Max Bacon, his crossed eyes or his motor bike.

"That was a close one, Henno," Brooks breathed. "Only for the Judge we could've been slaughtered."

15

A couple of weeks went by and there was no sign of Mad Max. It was the busy season in the market-gardening industry and he had taken time off to help his father. It was on most people's minds that it would be a good thing if he never reappeared.

Liz Finn certainly didn't seem to miss him, for she threw herself whole-heartedly into rehearsals for the show. Called *Rock Around Shylock*, it was going well. Even Mr King, the music teacher, a man hard to please at the best of times, seemed reasonably satisfied.

Hennessy had been promoted and given the part of Launcelot Gobbo, Shylock's clownish servant, while Brooks, to his immense delight, had achieved the status of Old Gobbo, Launcelot's father.

All during the Easter break they practised. As Easter was late, the April weather was too good for them to remain indoors and the cast sometimes moved across to the park opposite the school. There they provided free amusement for the passers-by, and occasioned an amount of jeering by the hooligans who frequented its wide open spaces.

Hennessy's grandmother was happy to see him involved but also a little nervous that he was neglecting his studies. To put her mind at rest he attended a cramming course during Easter week, working in the mornings and thus leaving himself free for afternoon rehearsals.

"You're becoming a model schoolboy," Pop told him, eyeing him suspiciously. He was probably a little disappointed: secretly he had enjoyed his grandson's escapades, finding them a cause of some excitement in the even routine of his days.

Hennessy and Brooks had their big scene early on in the show—a comic turn where much was made of the fact that Old Gobbo didn't recognise his own son and the son made gentle fun of the father. They had to do a dance and Hennessy sang a song with the refrain based on the theme that it takes a wise father to know his own child.

The dance was the problem, for Brooks was so clumsy that he kept falling over his feet. They tried it again and again but Brooks just couldn't get it right.

"What more can I do?" he asked plaintively after yet another bout of sweat-inducing activity. "Michael Jackson I'll never be."

"You can say that again. In spades."

"Can we try one more time?"

They went through the routine again, a few simple steps then a low bow to the audience. Once again Brooks got entangled in his feet and fell over.

Hennessy gazed down at him in dismay; then he saw the funny side of it and burst out laughing.

"Aw, come on," Brooks complained, "don't kick me when I'm down."

He looked close to tears.

"Wait a minute... Say that again..."

"Say what?"

"What you just said. It may be the answer to all our problems."

"What d'you mean?"

"Well, this is supposed to be a comic turn, isn't it? Supposing I did kick you? Just as you bend over. It'd be good for a laugh or two, and it'd tie in with your clumsiness..."

"Thanks very much."

"Let's try it."

They went through the dance again, with Hennessy encouraging his partner to exaggerate his awkwardness. Then, as they did their bow, Hennessy delivered a mighty kick to Brooks's ample backside and caused him to fall over with a roar.

"That's it," Hennessy said triumphantly. "We'll do it like that. It'll bring the house down."

That evening they showed it to Mr King and, after some initial reluctance, he agreed to it. Brooks, in spite of the probability of a sore bum, was over the moon.

Hennessy, however, was not too pleased about another bit of business he was forced into against his will. In order to make Lancelot's appearance as ridiculous as possible, Mr King asked him to try and think of something to cause the audience to laugh as soon as he made his entrance.

In the teacher's presence—and Hennessy could

have killed his friend for suggesting it—Brooks came up with the idea of Gobbo's having a parrot on his shoulder.

"A parrot? Where would he get a parrot?" Kinger asked.

"He already has one," Brooks told him. "Or at least his grandparents do. It'd be just right."

"Is this true?" the teacher asked a glowering Hennessy.

Reluctantly he had to admit that it was true, and so it was settled that when he came for the next rehearsal he would bring Mabel along as well.

In spite of his arguments to dissuade her, Molly also thought the idea a good one: "Poor old Mabel," she said. "She never gets any excitement. This'll perk her up, bring the smile back to her face..."

So it was settled and Hennessy trudged off to his room with the expression of the condemned man about to face the executioner's axe.

16

The day of the dress rehearsal dawned and everyone, including Mr King, was on tenterhooks.

To cut costs, the members of the cast had been asked to provide their own costumes and, when Hennessy told Molly, she immediately decided that he should wear a suit of motley.

"A suit of what?"

"Of motley. I'll show you what I mean."

She hurried away and then came back with a large, leather-bound book. She opened it at a particular page and he gazed with no little distaste at a figure in a tunic and tight breeches and wearing a pixie hat with two little horns sticking out of it.

"You must be joking!"

"That's what the court jester looked like in those days," Molly informed him. "I could run up a suit like that for you with no bother..."

"Well, don't bother."

True to her word, however, on the evening of the great day she presented him with the suit, which stitched together out of squares of different coloured cloths looked as iridescent as a rainbow.

"If I wear that I'll be laughed out of the hall," Hennessy protested.

"Well, isn't that what you want? After all, you are supposed to be a clown."

He conceded that, took the suit away to his room and put it on. With the hat, he felt he looked ridiculous but without it, merely funny. He decided he'd compromise: he'd lose the pixie but wear the tunic and breeches.

After an initial burst of laughter, the rest of the cast told him he looked great and Kinger was chuffed.

"With that, and the parrot on your shoulder, you really look the part," he told him. "I wish some of the others had gone to the same trouble…"

Numbered among some of the others was Brooks. He had simply cut a hole in a large grey blanket and stuck his head through. The blanket was shedding and it gave off a distinct smell of old dog.

"Don't come too close to me wearing that thing," Hennessy warned him. "It's already after eating two of the page boys."

But Brooks was too nervous to pay any heed to him. So were most of the rest of the cast. There was a lot of horse-play and high-pitched laughter, but underneath it there was an unease that caused glances to be furtive and cigarettes to be smoked as if they were going out of fashion.

While the stage crew was getting things ready, Hennessy caught Brooks's eye and motioned to him to follow him out to the jakes. They pushed through the door, and to Brooks's amazement, Hennessy ushered him into one of the cubicles. In order to make room for the two of them, Brooks had to sit on the toilet.

"I hope no one comes in and finds us here," he said. "We'd never live it down..."

"Don't mind that. I want to ask you a question."

"What is it?"

Before answering, Hennessy levered himself up by his hands until he was looking out over the door. Satisfied that there was no one else about, he let himself down again.

"What d'you think of Mercedes McGurk in the part of Portia?" he asked in a whisper.

"I think she's very good," Brooks replied, also in a whisper.

"You don't thing she's a bit stiff?"

"Maybe... But she's got a great voice."

"I think Liz Finn'd do the part better."

"What?"

"I think she'd be ace as Portia."

"I heard you the first time. But it's a bit late for that, isn't it?"

"She's been the understudy from the start. She knows the part inside out."

"Maybe she does, but McGurk is not likely to give it up to her now."

"I know that. But supposing on the night McGurk doesn't turn up?"

"Why wouldn't she?"

Once again Hennessy went through his chin-up routine on the door. The coast was still clear.

Avoiding Brooks's eye he said, "I could make it

happen that she doesn't."

"How?"

"Well, I've been watching her and I've noticed that before every rehearsal she goes off to one of the classrooms to warm up her voice. Now on Sunday night if someone were to lock the door behind her and cause her to be late, why Liz Finn'd have to take over, wouldn't she?"

Brooks looked shocked.

"You wouldn't..." he breathed.

"Oh yes, I would."

"You'd do that for Liz Finn after the trouble she got you into with Maxie Bacon?"

"Ah, don't mind that. I like her, and if I do this for her it'd kind of tip the odds in my favour. I know how badly she wants the part."

Brooks pushed himself up off the toilet bowl.

"I'm getting outa here," he said. "I'm going to have nothing to do with this."

"No, wait a minute." Hennessy pushed him back onto the seat. "Hear me out. All I want you to do is to let her out after the first act. Liz'd be well into the part by then and it wouldn't matter if she appeared..."

"Why me?" Brooks said indignantly. "Why don't you let her out yourself?"

"Well, everyone knows I'm soft on Liz Finn... I'd be the first suspect. But if it was you... You've got an innocent face, no one'd suspect you."

"How would I know which room she'd be in?"

"I've thought of that. What I'll do is, I'll lock all the rooms except one, then she'll have to go in there."

"Where'll you get the keys?"

"There's only one, the master key. I borrowed Harry the caretaker's when he wasn't looking and made an impression in a bar of soap. It was easy to get one cut."

"I don't believe you."

"Cross my heart and hope to die."

"I thought that only worked in the movies."

"Well, it worked for me."

Brooks sighed, his chin on his hand. It was obvious he didn't like it, but it was also obvious that he was going to do it.

"Good man," Hennessy encouraged him, "you're a real brick."

"As thick as one, you mean."

Furtively Hennessy opened the door of the cubicle and glanced about. "We'd better stop meeting in here," he said. "You know how people talk."

Brooks rolled his eyes to the ceiling but said nothing.

At seven-thirty the orchestra struck up. It consisted of O'Brien and his merry band and two serious-looking girls, one on violin, one on flute. A self-styled professional named Puff O'Grady had been brought in to monitor the sound: he was large and fat and he sat behind his flashing deck feeding his face and drinking one can of beer after another. Upon seeing him, Brooks gave it as his opinion that when the sound got loud enough, Puff would explode.

Young Gobbo and Old Gobbo had their big scene in Act Two and, while they waited, Hennessy tried to make conversation with Liz Finn. She was wearing a long flowered dress with padded shoulders and she'd dyed her hair bright red.

"I like the hair," he told her, almost biting his tongue.

"Got it done special. Three hours it took to get it that colour. I thought purple first, but red's better..."

Better than what? Hennessy wondered, but aloud he said,"Yeah, it's certainly...eh...unusual. Usually Jews have black hair, though."

"Get away?"

"And big noses."

Liz made a face, then resumed chewing her gum. She jigged about to the music, moving her shoulders up and down. "What's he wearing then?" she asked, indicating Brooks. "He looks as if he's crawling out of a bush."

"He's Old Gobbo."

"He's a gob alright, a gobdaw..."

The first scene ended and Antonio and his friends came into the wings, streaming with sweat. The rest of them stood back to allow Portia and her maid, Nerissa, through.

"Lookit the set of her," Liz Finn growled, loud enough for Mercedes McGurk to hear."You'd think she was Lady Muck..."

The McGurk girl was small and slim, with a pretty face and short wavy black hair. As she passed Liz Finn she made clucking sounds with her lips, then she said, "Sticks and stones, Lizzie…The hair should be green though, green for envy."

"Did you hear that?" Liz said. "The cheek of her…"

Hennessy had to admit, however, that she had an excellent singing voice. And she wasn't half bad at the acting either. When Liz's turn came she showed herself to be pretty wooden, and she had a high reedy voice that disappeared into the rafters when she struck a high note. He began to wonder if his little scheme of replacing one for the other was such a bright idea after all.

Finally his and Brooks's turn came and they pranced out onto the stage, he with Mabel on his shoulder, Brooks in his evil smelling blanket. They got through their song okay but, when the time came for him to deliver the kick to Brooks's gable end, the parrot decided to take a hand—or a beak, to be more exact.

Fulfilling all Hennessy's worst expectations, Mabel gave a screech, rose high in the air, then dive-bombed Brooks as he was bending over. Getting a good grip with her claws, she began pecking rat-a-tat-tat like a woodpecker with the hiccups.

With a yell, Brooks straightened up, clasped both hands to the afflicted area and began running around the stage. The music kept in tune with his frantic progress, the synthesiser echoing his howls. Then the rest of the cast, not wishing to be left out, came crowding out of the wings, clapping their hands and laughing their heads off.

The only one not amused was Mr King. He came rushing up the aisle, bald head and glasses gleaming, waving his script like a club. Unfortunately for him, just as he arrived at the stage Mabel let go of Brooks's rear end and spotting another likely victim zoomed off in his direction.

If he had trotted up the aisle, Kinger positively galloped back down it. Like a steeplechaser he vaulted the bench he'd been sitting on, just made it to the door ahead of the parrot, disappeared through and slammed it after him.

Mabel, deprived of her prey, flew around the room a couple of times, then alighted on one of the cross beams of the ceiling. As though to make one final statement, she dropped her business on the heads of a couple of onlookers who were unfortunate enough to be standing beneath her.

So ended Mabel's brief taste of stardom. Kinger absolutely refused to have her round the place again, much to Hennessy's relief. She was put back in her cage, a coat was draped over it, and she was left to give out to herself for the rest of the night.

The dress rehearsal ambled on, everything now an anticlimax after the attack of the lunatic parrot. The only other event of note was that near the end Puff O'Grady passed out from all the beer he had drunk, slumped forward onto his monitor board and blew every fuse in the house.

By the time that Hennessy had got out of his costume, everyone else had gone. Harry the porter was impatient to lock up and be off, and he hurried Hennessy out, complaining that the pubs would all be closed before he got there.

Outside it was raining, a light mist that swirled and eddied in the yellow glow of the traffic. Hennessy hunched his shoulders as he walked, his bag in one hand, Mabel in her cage dangling from the other. He was making for the bus stop when he suddenly noticed the bulky figure on the motor bike, motionless, the rain slick on the black leather, the visor of the helmet closed and dark.

He slowed down, a tremor of apprehension invading his mind. Don't be silly, he told himself, there must be thousands of bikers in Dublin, no reason to believe that this was Max Bacon lying in wait for him.

Taking no chances, however, he moved to the edge of the path and waited for a break in traffic to cross the road. Immediately the motor bike engine came to shattering life, and the headlight cut through the rain in a blaze of brilliance.

Hennessy backed up until he could feel the iron railing of the park against his back. There was no one else about, the pathway deserted. He could make for the bus stop, but he would have to pass the figure on the bike to get to it.

His only alternative was to run as fast as he could in the opposite direction but after his experience of trying to outrun the motor bike he didn't see much joy in that.

There was no doubt in his mind now that it was

Mad Max and that if he didn't get out of there fast he'd soon be merely a stain on the pavement. Waiting no longer he vaulted the railing and landed on the grass of the park. At least in here there would be bushes and trees that would form obstacles for the machine.

He took off, his feet slipping in the soft ground and Mabel protesting at the jolting she was receiving. His best hope was to keep close to the railing, move further down and get out near the bus stop. At the back of the park was the railway line, a high wall preventing people from climbing out onto it and the Tolka river bordered it in the direction he was heading.

He ran, his heart thumping in his chest, the rain and the heavy going slowing his progress. Blundering into a flower bed, he fell over, lost his bag, scrabbled about for it, and then gave it up as a lost cause. He went on, his head telling him he was being silly but the rest of him in a state of panic that communicated itself to his anxious, hurrying feet.

He came to a clump of trees and leaned against the trunk of one to get his breath back. Not too far from him the traffic rumbled on unconcernedly, but here in the park there was a stillness that was almost sinister. When he strained his ears he could hear rustlings and shufflings, as though small animals with sharp teeth were converging on him from all sides. It was a Stephen King world in here, the darkness full of menace and objects that in daylight would have looked ordinary now taking on weird and threatening shapes.

Still, the darkness was far preferable to the blinding beam of light that suddenly appeared from nowhere and spotlighted him against the tree. It was accompanied by the stuttering reverberation of the motor bike engine, the rider indistinct but huge behind the blare of light.

Hennessy darted around to the other side of the tree. Then he threw caution to the wind and took off again. The headlight playing on his back made him feel that the machine itself was only a matter of inches behind him and the roaring clatter it made heightened the effect. He imagined it knocking him down, could feel the pressure of the wheels as they passed over him, saw himself sinking into the ground, could taste the coldness of clay and wet leaves.

Instinctively he began to swerve, taking a zig-zag course, his feet slipping and sliding. His greatest fear was of falling, and he knew that if that were to happen he'd be finished. Mad Max would be on him and there'd be bits of him all over the park come morning.

He ran on, the breath whistling in his throat, and, when it was too late, he saw the obstacle looming up in front of him. He had come upon it so quickly that he didn't have time to do anything but try to hurdle it. Jump, he told himself, and that was exactly what he did, springboarding up in the air, out and over.

At the height of his leap, for one timeless moment, he felt as if he were treading the very air, his arms whirling, his legs bicycling. But what goes up must come down, and when he was through the apex of his jump his descent began.

He flinched, trying to fold himself into a ball as he awaited impact, but when it came it was an anti-climax. Instead of a hard, unyielding surface, it was a heaving, glutinous, sticky sea of mud that he plopped into, driving down into it so that he was immersed to the waist, his downward progress halted and the wind knocked out of him.

He stayed like that—he had no choice in the matter—gulping great mouthfuls of wet air, relieved to have suffered such a soft landing, happy as a pig in muck.

He didn't have to be a genius to know what had happened: he had vaulted the wall of the park and landed in the Tolka river, a river that was luckily at low tide. Hopefully he wondered if Bacon too had hit the wall and had been catapulted into the river, but there was no sound of anyone else splashing about near at hand. He was probably already on his way home, convinced that his enemy had been swallowed up, never to be seen again.

That's what you think, Maxie, Hennessy thought grimly, but just wait. I'll get out of this, and when I do you'll need an army to keep me away from you.

Cautiously he tensed his legs, and was relieved to feel bottom under his feet. He began to inch his way backward, the mud squelching and wobbling like blancmange. However it didn't smell like blanc-mange, rather it had a stench as though an ass-load of O'Brien's football socks had been mashed, made into a paste and spread thickly along the river bottom.

He was almost to the bank when he heard a small, forlorn voice suddenly ask, "What's for tea? What's for tea?" It was Mabel the parrot somewhere out in the darkness, possibly slowly sinking into the morass.

For a moment he was tempted to leave her there but then he thought of Molly and how she'd skin him alive if he returned without the bird. Resignedly he made his way forward again and soon found the cage with his clutching fingers. He brought it to him and sensed rather than saw Mabel inside it.

In spite of himself, he began to feel a twinge of affection for the moth-eaten relic. They had gone through a lot together: an attack of pig slurry, being chased by Mad Max and his mechanical monster and a great leap out into the unknown. Now here they were, both of them up to their armpits in smelly splodge, standing in the middle of a river with the rain belting down on them. Could any two have suffered more?

With that, Mabel stuck her head out between the bars of the cage and fastened her beak on Hennessy's nose in a grip that a strong man with a pliers would have envied.

17

At eleven o'clock that night a most singular figure was to be seen trudging up the North Circular Road. The rain had stopped and the moon was out but the apparition paid no heed to his surroundings.

To the eye of a beholder it might have appeared that some mad sculptor had imitated Dr Frankenstein and had made one of his creations come alive. There was an unfinished air about him, but with a burnishing and a lump knocked off here and there, he might have passed muster as an example of prehistoric man—but only just. There was also a decided stench about him, as though he had inadvertently fallen into a cesspit.

No one stayed long enough to form any such opinions, however, for as soon as he appeared people took off like startled jackrabbits. Two teenaged girls, returning from town having seen the horror film *Friday the 13th V*, ran off screaming at his approach, an elderly lady attacked him with her umbrella and the conductor of a bus that he attempted to board informed him that if he so much as set foot on his platform he'd brain him with his ticket dispenser.

Hennessy—for it was indeed he—continued on his sad and lonesome way. The joy of having escaped from Max Bacon had long since worn off and all he wanted now was a hot bath and the warm harbour of his sleeping-bag. Only an old tramp gave him any kind of civil greeting, recognising in him no doubt a fellow knight of the road as down on his luck as himself.

With a groan of relief he finally made the house on the North Circular Road. Never had he been so glad to see it. Mabel, too, perked up, beginning again her refrain of "What's for tea? What's for tea?"

The caked mud had hardened so much that he was unable to get his hand into his pocket for his key, so he had to ring the bell. When the light came on over the door he looked down at himself. Half the bed of the Tolka river was stuck to him. His clothes were ruined. He smelled like a sack of month-old fish. And he had an itch in the middle of his back that he had no possible way of getting at.

The door opened and his grandfather stood looking out at him. After a moment for reflection he said, "My God, it's the mummy, straight from the tomb. I had a feeling this would happen to me since I started using that bloody metal detector..."

"Very funny."

"An English-speaking mummy at that. Have you come to put the curse of the undead on me?"

Hennessy stood in the middle of the hallway, shedding mud. He tried to drop the parrot cage but it was firmly fixed to his hand; like that character in Greek mythology with the rock on his back, he'd probably have to traipse around for the rest of his natural with Mabel hanging out of him.

"Scratch my back, Pop," he implored his grandfather. "I've got an itch that's driving me crazy."

"I'll scratch your back if you scratch mine. Promise you won't put your curse on me?"

"Yes, yes, only hurry up."

Pop got an umbrella from the hallstand and began rubbing the handle of it up and down Hennessy's back. While he was doing this his wife's voice called, "Who is it, Caskey? Is it Michael?"

"I'm not too sure," Pop answered, vigorously working the handle of the brolly. "It talks with his voice but it doesn't look much like him. Come to think of it, it doesn't look much like anything at all."

"What's that you say?"

"Come and see for yourself, woman. It's either him or the Creature from the Black Lagoon."

Molly appeared, but even her laid-back personality couldn't accept Hennessy's sea-change without a double-take and a gasp or two.

"What in God's name..?"

"I can explain," her grandson told her, taking a step forward and causing her to back-pedal. "Mabel got out of her cage and flew into the park. I followed her. It was dark and before I knew what was happening both of us had fallen into the river. Could have happened to a bishop..."

"A bishop?"

"Well..." Hennessy raised his arm and there was a creaking sound as if something needed oiling. "The tide was out," he went on, "and I fell into the mud. It took me ages to get out. I tried to get the stuff off me but it's like glue. Now it's dried out and I feel as if I'm encased in plaster of Paris."

"Doesn't smell like plaster of Paris," Pop said, wrinkling his nose.

"Oh, be quiet, Caskey," his wife told him. "Can't you see the poor boy's in a terrible state? And all because of Mabel..."

All three of them gazed at the thing in the cage, which looked miserably back at them.

"That's right," Hennessy said, nodding and causing another shower of dried mud to rat-a-tat-tat onto the carpet. "I knew how devastated you'd be if I came home without her..."

To give Molly her due, she asked no more questions. After a brief struggle, she managed to wrest Mabel's cage away from her grandson, the bird complaining that she was banjaxed. Then Pop was dispatched to find a sheet of plastic which was spread on the bathroom floor. Hennessy stood on it and peeled off his mud-stiffened clothes. He then shoved the whole lot out the door for Pop to take away, got into the bath and in no time at all was soaping, scrubbing and singing at the top of his voice.

He was not one to fret for long over past misfortunes, knowing only too well that there were new ones lying in wait for him just around the corner. Like a rubber ball, he knew how to bounce...

18

It was the first night of *Rock Around Shylock* and all that day the cast members had been as irritable as cats on hot tin roofs. Brooks was so bad that he even puffed on a cigarette to calm his nerves, a performance so weirdly wonderful that he caused everyone around, including himself, to choke: he from the smoke, the others with laughter.

Hennessy went out of his way to stay in Mercedes McGurk's company, following her about, asking her if he could do anything for her, smiling, talking, offering to carry her books.

"What's wrong with you?" she asked him finally. "You look and sound as if you've been at the magic mushrooms."

Hennessy did his best to look hurt.

"I'm only trying to make sure you're relaxed," he told her. "Everyone else looks as if they're walking on eggshells. It's no joke having such an important part. The whole show revolves around you. If anything were to happen to you...well..."

He spread his hands and shrugged his shoulders.

The girl tossed her head. "Nothing's going to happen to me, and if I'm jumpy it's because you're making me nervous. Why don't you go off and join your own friends? I've never noticed you being that pally with me before."

"That's because I'm shy. I've been worshipping you from afar..."

"In a pig's eye?"

The girl looked closely at him, then she grinned. "You're beginning a pimple on the end of your nose, d'you know that? It's all red and shiny. Is it sore, I hope?"

Aha, Hennessy thought: this was what he had hoped for, the girl doing or saying something nasty so that he wouldn't be sorry about what he was going to do to her. It'd help to keep his conscience in check, silence the small voice that kept saying inside his head. "It's not right what you're about to cause to happen to this girl. It's unworthy of you, a terrible, terrible thing that you'll regret for the rest of your life..."

As the dreaded hour drew nearer, nervousness spread like an invisible fog. The cast had gathered in the prefab block behind the school to have their make-up applied and the painted faces that began to appear helped to relieve the tension.

Brooks gave himself a moustache that curled up his face like a rat's tail and painted his mouth with bright red lipstick. People kept coming up to him, pouting their lips and saying, "Give us a kiss."

In the middle of the hubbub he leaned over to Hennessy and asked him if he still intended going ahead with his plan.

"Will you keep it down for crying out loud," he

replied, glancing about anxiously. He had already been over to the main school building and locked all the rooms except 6b on the second floor. While actually doing it he had experienced misgivings, but when he returned the sight of Liz Finn in a long white dress had stifled his doubts. She looked like the bee's knees.

"What?" she had mouthed at him, as he told her just that.

"You look like a million dollars. Dresses suit you."

"I feel a right ninny. This thing is like a sack."

At half-past seven Mr King came in and called for silence. He had obviously entered into the spirit of being a producer, for he was wearing a Fair Isle sweater that positively glowed. As well a beret was tipped over one ear and he was smoking a cigarette in a long holder.

He was greeted by wolf-whistles and a few jeers but gradually silence descended under the command of his upraised hands.

"Now, as this is our first night," he told them, "we're bound to make a few mistakes. If one of you dries, then listen for the prompter. The secret is to keep going at all costs. And don't be looking for your friends and relations in the audience. If I see anyone waving or winking, I'll swing for them. And when you're off-stage, don't be talking and kicking up a row. You can be heard out in the hall, remember. That's about it. If you've got any problems, you'd better get them ironed out now. We'll try and start as close to eight as possible. Good luck and break a leg..."

There was a muted cheer and then the noise level began to rise again. As Mr King went into conference with his leading man, Hennessy kept an eye on Mercedes McGurk. And she was worth keeping an eye on. Like Liz she too was wearing a long dress, only hers was blue. And she knew something about make-up, for her face looked just right. She had used eye shadow cleverly to bring out the sparkle in her eyes and, he had to admit, she too looked like the bee's knees.

Still, when she made her move and slipped quietly out the door, he followed after a reasonable interval. He was wearing a raincoat over his jester's costume, which Molly had had to remake to replace the one he'd lost in the park, but his made-up face aroused quite an amount of interest in the hangers-on who were loitering about waiting to encourage or jeer their friends in the cast.

He tiptoed, Pink Panther fashion, around the back of the school building. The evening was still bright, the sky a pale shade of blue and the sun a glare of brilliance low on the horizon. He was looking back over his shoulder, with the consequence that he ran straight into the wall, a painful collision that did nothing to enhance the beauty of his already red and shiny nose.

Before going in the door he looked about him once more. The coast seemed clear. He faced about and, framed in the doorway and looking as furtive as himself, was Mr House, the Principal.

It was difficult to say which of them was the more startled. They both reared backwards; flight was contemplated, then rejected. Feeling for some reason that it was called for, Hennessy put out his hand, grasped the Principal's and shook it vigorously.

"What..? Oh, yes..."

Mr House dithered, escape still obviously on his mind. He looked down at his hand, still clasped in Hennessy's, then hurriedly withdrew it as though he'd been stung. He put it behind his back and possibly fearing that the other one was also in danger, he put it behind his back as well.

"Eh...I forgot something," Hennessy stammered. "Yes, that's right, I left my script in my locker..."

"Locker?" Mr House murmured, bewilderment in his eyes.

"No, not locker. In my desk. I left my script in my desk and now I need it. The script that is, not the desk. I've forgotten some of my lines. Need to look them up..."

"Up?"

"Learn them, I mean. Well relearn them actually. I'm Launcelot Gobbo..."

"Oh, so nice to meet you. House is my name."

He went to put out his hand, then thought better of it. Instead he gave a little bow.

"That's my name in the play," Hennessy explained, desperate to be gone but held in spite of himself. He had the distinct impression of being caught in a giant roll of flypaper.

"Play?"

"The musical. *Rock Around Shylock.*"

"Yes, that's it," Mr House said but he didn't look convinced. "But I musn't keep you, Mr...Ah...Gobbo? Things to be done you know. Always something to be attended to..."—he gave an apologetic little laugh— "No rest for the wicked...Eh?"

"I suppose not."

"Yes...Well..."

With a sidestep, Mr House took his leave, with Hennessy staring after him, his mouth open. The man was like a will-o'-the-wisp: it was a wonder he hadn't disappeared in a puff of smoke.

Hennessy continued on his mission of intrigue, pitty-patting up the stairs, his raincoat flapping. The eyes of the footballers in the photographs hung slanting up the stairwell wall seemed to follow his progress—those manly fellows who had given their all, and then some, for the greater honour and glory of the old school. As he watched out of the corner of his eye, all their faces began to frown disapprovingly at him. Go back, Henno, they seemed to say, don't do this terrible thing.

Shaking his head to dispel such fancies, he bounded along. The top corridor was shadowed and dim, the doors all closed. Swallowing hard, he crept along to 6b and put his ear to the woodwork. Slightly muffled, the sound of Mercedes McGurk sending her voice up and down the scale came to him. With trembling fingers he inserted the stolen key and turned it in the lock. To his fevered imagination the tumblers made a crack like a pistol going off.

He turned and fled along the length of the corridor and down the stairs. He was out of breath by the time he got to the ground floor, but he didn't pause. He had to get out, leave the scene of his crime, put it behind him. With a feeling of relief akin to someone climbing out of a snake-pit, he took hold of the knob of the front door and prepared to turn it.

Nothing happened. The knob wouldn't turn. The door was locked.

"I don't believe this," he muttered, bending down to get a better look at what was wrong. But there was nothing wrong; it was merely that the door was securely fastened.

Once again he fumbled the master key out of his pocket, put it in the keyhole and waggled it about. It turned okay, but the door still wouldn't open. It was then that he remembered the mortice lock, how he had often seen Harry the caretaker use two keys to barricade the front door. Someone—most probably Mr House in his forgetful way—had locked the door without checking first to see if there was anyone inside. And the problem was that, as all the windows were double-glazed and locked also, he now had no way of getting out.

Hennessy leaned against the wall and took a number of deep breaths. He couldn't help but feel that this was a form of punishment for what he had just done to Mercedes McGurk. Now, as a kind of cosmic joke, both of them were imprisoned.

As he stood feeling sorry for himself, a muffled sound began to beat its way into his troubled consciousness. For a second he was puzzled, then he realised it was the girl in the room above him banging on the door. She too had discovered her predicament.

Wearily he once more ascended the stairs, made his way along the corridor and turned the key in the lock of room 6b. The girl inside, not realising that it was now unlocked, continued banging on the door.

"It's open," Hennessy suddenly roared, frustration welling up in him like a tidal wave.

There was a pause, then the handle turned and the door slowly moved inwards. An eye was applied to the gap.

Hennessy spread his hands, did a little dance and sang, "Tar ra, tar ra."

Mercedes opened the door wider and gazed at him. "Oh, it's you," she said. "I was locked in."

"I know."

"Yes, I suppose you would, seeing as you let me out."

"No, I know because I did it."

"Did what?"

"Locked you in."

The girl looked puzzled: "No, you let me out."

"But I locked you in in the first place."

"Why would you do that?"

Hennessy, beginning to think well of himself again because he'd cleared his conscience, admitted: "I didn't want you starring in the play. I wanted Liz Finn to have the part of Portia."

"I see."

"You do?"

"Yes, it's a natural thing to want your girlfriend to have the best part."

"But not the way I went about it, surely?"

"I suppose your intentions were good...Towards her, anyway."

"She doesn't know anything about it, mind. And she's not my girlfriend. Not really..."

"She's not?"

"No, she's not."

Hennessy gazed at the girl, still standing in the open door: "I can't put this together," he told her. "I can't...I can't understand why you're not mad at me. It's not natural..."

"Oh, I didn't say I wasn't mad at you," the girl said, stepping forward. "Let me show you just how mad at you I am..."

Without warning, she suddenly swung at Hennessy, her open palm whip-cracking against his jaw. Surprise, as well as the momentum of it, drove him backwards, his heels slid on the polished floor, his legs went up in the air, and he sat down with an unmerciful thump.

Through stinging eyes he saw Mercedes put her hand to her face, then snort with laughter. She looked away from him, but her shoulders continued to shake.

"Boy, that hurt," he told her, then after a moment's consideration he admitted: "But I guess I deserved it..."

"Of course you deserved it. But now that it's done, I'm ready to be friends. I don't believe in holding grudges."

"Neither do I."

The girl again put out her hand, but this time it was to help Hennessy up.

"You certainly pack a wallop," he told her. "How'd you learn to hit like that?"

"I've four brothers. It's a question of fight your corner or go under."

They stared at one another, both of them suddenly embarrassed. It showed itself in Mercedes as a crinkle-eyed, Ellen Barkin grin that she kept turning her face away to hide, while Hennessy hung his head in an "aw, shucks" manner, did his familiar shifting from foot to foot and admitted that they were locked in.

"Well, how're we going to get out of here?" she said. "It must be nearly time for the show to start. They're probably looking for us, so let's think of some way of attracting their attention. We could switch the lights on and off, that might do it."

Hennessy shook his head. "It's too bright. They wouldn't see them. I've got a better idea. There's one window that isn't double-glazed and locked. It's in the boys' toilet. It's pretty small, but I think I can get through it and out on to the roof. Come on..."

Without thinking he took the girl's hand and they ran down the corridor. At the door of the toilet she hesitated but then she followed him in.

The window had frosted glass in it and was over the row of sinks. It took Hennessy an amount of effort before he was able to push it open: it creaked and groaned but finally gave.

"I don't know if you'll get through there," Mercedes told him. "It looks pretty narrow to me."

Hennessy was inclined to agree with her, but was reluctant to give in too easily. He hoisted himself up, gripping the window frame and looked out. The flat roof of the cloakroom was below him but it seemed an awful long way down.

"I'll have to get out feet first," he said. "Then I'll drop down onto the roof below."

"You're either very brave or just plain nuts..."

"Probably the second," Hennessy agreed. "My first problem though, is how to get out. It's going to be a tight squeeze."

"Maybe if you stripped off and greased yourself with soap?"

"I'll treat that suggestion with the respect it deserves," Hennessy said.

He blew a raspberry.

Pulling himself up until his nose was against the ceiling, he manoeuvred his feet and legs through the narrow aperture. His hips became wedged but, after a deal of wriggling about, he managed to get them unstuck.

"Careful," the girl said behind him. All she could see of him now were his arms and the top of his head.

"Count to three," he ordered her.

She did as he asked and, when she got to the third number, he took a deep breath, let go and with a roar of "Geronimo" disappeared from her view. There was a long pause before she heard a thud and a distant cry of pain.

Hennessy landed hard on the felt covered roof, then rolled in the best tradition of the stunt men he'd often seen in films. Trouble was, he overdid it, went head over heels to the very edge, then felt himself being launched into space. In desperation he crooked his fingers and, as he passed by, managed to hook them into the metal rainwater chute. His body swung out, stopped abruptly, then whammed back into the wall. The breath was driven from his lungs and he almost let go but some instinct of self-preservation made him hold on. The strain was terrific but then his scrabbling feet found purchase and he was able to ease the pull on his arms.

He paused for a moment of prayer and thanksgiving and listened to the tortured creaking of his muscles. He was sure that when he eventually got back to *terra firma* his knuckles would be dragging along the ground from the extension his arms had undergone.

His moment of reflection over, he hauled himself up and lay face down on the roof. The felt was hard and smelled of tar, but at that moment it could have been a bed of nails and he wouldn't have cared. He was just glad to be safely lying on it.

After a time he reluctantly stirred himself and applied his mind to finding a way down to the ground. He peered over the edge. He was up about twenty feet, give or take a few inches, but at the corner nearest to him he saw a drainpipe fixed to the wall. It wouldn't take much to shin down that.

He was about to do just that when he heard a

familiar voice call out to him from above. At first he thought he was imagining it, but then it came again, polite, slightly uneasy, but unmistakably the dulcet tones of the Principal, the one and only Mr House.

"I say...hello down there. Are you in some difficulty?"

Resignedly Hennessy looked up and saw the dreaded features gazing down at him from the same window that he'd exited from such a short time before.

"Oh, it's you...Ah, Gobbo...Have you lost something?"

For a moment Hennessy wondered at the man's remarkable train of thought that he should come to the conclusion that one of his pupils was standing on a roof because he had lost something. He was surely spaced out so far that he could have belonged to another galaxy.

"No, sir, I was locked in and was trying to get out..."

"Locked in? How extraordinary! Who could have possibly locked you in?"

"You, sir."

"Me?"

"You probably thought the building was empty."

"Did I?"

"I guess so."

"Quite. Well, we'll have to see if we can procure a ladder or something and get you down. You stay there and I'll see what can be done..."

The face at the window disappeared and, as soon

as it did, Hennessy scurried over to the corner of the roof, caught hold of the drainpipe and went down it like a scalded cat. When he hit the ground his feet were already running and he was around the back of the school and galloping in the direction of the hall before Housey had even emerged from the main door.

19

The first person Hennessy encountered when he slipped in the side door of the hall was Mercedes McGurk. She was standing in the wings looking quite composed, watching Antonio and Bassanio do the cakewalk against a garishly-painted backdrop of downtown Venice. Audience reaction sounded loud and energetic.

"How'd you get out?" he hissed, clutching at her arm.

"I heard Housey coming in, so I just stood behind a door, waited for him to pass and, hey presto, I was out and away. I tried to warn you but you were hanging about a bit at the time and I didn't think you'd want to be disturbed. Did he see you?"

Hennessy breathed hard.

"He did. And at this very moment he's looking for a ladder to get me down."

"Don't worry about it. By the time he's out the door he'll have forgotten what he was going to do. His brain's like a sieve. Everything falls through it."

"I suppose you're right."

"Of course I am. Look on it all as a bit of crack. That's what I'm doing."

Suddenly Hennessy remembered Brooks. He was

probably already on his way over to release Mercedes, thinking she was still locked in. He could well blunder into a situation that he wouldn't be able to handle.

Muttering a quick goodbye to the girl, Hennessy scooted once more out the door and prepared to break into a gallop. He was halted in his tracks, however, by the sight that greeted him outside. Carrying a ladder between them almost as reverently as a coffin, Brooks and Harry the caretaker were marching in stately procession behind the figure of Mr House. It was obvious that the school principal had commandeered them and that they were on their way to get Hennessy down from his supposed perch on the roof.

In spite of himself, Hennessy started laughing. The whole business was just too funny for words and now this scene from a silent film comedy capped it all? Brooks in his blanket and made-up face, Harry with his hair parted down the middle and a nose like a beacon and Housey tripping over himself in front of them—they were a comic turn walking right out of the past.

His first impulse was to take up a position in the rear and, imitating their funereal pace, step it out all the way across the yard behind them. The whole scene reminded him of those stories one heard of people reading their own obituaries in the newspapers.

Reluctantly abandoning this idea, he retraced his steps, ran quickly around the front of the school and was in place to meet the little parade when it arrived at the main block.

Mr House looked at him and was preparing to pass by when his eyes suddenly narrowed suspiciously. He stopped abruptly, and Harry nudged the end of the ladder into him from behind.

Housey gave a little jump, a mere lifting of the shoulders as though some invisible force had tried to pick him up. The procession halted and three pairs of eyes gazed at Hennessy, one pair bemused, the other two murderous. Explanations were obviously called for.

"I climbed down the drainpipe," Hennessy said lamely, gesturing at the front of the building.

The three pairs of eyes swung away from him and stared in the direction he was pointing, then they rounded on him again. Even Mr House's meek stare was beginning to evaporate into something approaching sternness.

"How'd you get up on the roof?" Harry the caretaker inquired, in a tone that suggested that whatever answer he got he wouldn't be prepared to believe it.

"I climbed out through the toilet window."

"Why?"

"I was locked in."

"You could've broken your neck"—this time the tone implied that if such an event had occurred Harry, for one, wouldn't have rushed into mourning.

"Yes...Ah..." Mr House gestured aimlessly. "All's well that ends well, I suppose. No need now for that ladder, men..."

He gazed at the sky, the ground, his fingernails.

He shuffled his feet, he cleared his throat. It was clear he wished to bring their little confab to an end but wasn't too sure how to go about doing it.

Harry took him out of his misery by first letting out a string of curses and then doing an about-turn with the ladder that nearly took the heads off the other three. He marched off, the end of it dragging along the ground and making a statement noisily behind him.

"His evening off," Mr House explained by way of excuse. "Doesn't like to be bothered..."

He paused and seemed to go into a trance, giving Brooks the opportunity to nudge Hennessy painfully in the ribs.

"What about the girl?" he hissed, the lipstick making his lips look as if they were glued together.

"What girl?"

"McGurk. The one you locked in the school and that I was supposed to let out."

"She's already out. It's a long story. Remind me to tell it to you when I've an hour or twenty to spare..."

While they were whispering, Mr House had begun to edge away, clearly with the intention of making good his escape while their attention was elsewhere. When he saw them looking at him he again became fidgety.

"Well...That'll be all then," he said, flapping his hands at them dismissively. "Storm in a teacup...Eh, Gobbo?"

"Gobbo?" Brooks said, his eyes wild.

Unable to resist the urge to stir things up one

more time, Hennessy said, "I'd like you to meet my father, Old Gobbo, sir. He and I do a double-act, song and dance…"

Mr House gazed despairingly at Brooks.

"Is that so? Music-hall, no doubt?"

"We're top of the bill…"

"For God's sake, Henno," Brooks implored, backing away and striving to keep a sickly grin on his painted visage.

"Well, I guess we have to go now," Hennessy said, relenting. "Sorry I put you to so much trouble, sir. The ladder and all…"

With an expression of immense relief, Mr House gave them what amounted to a blessing.

"Not at all, not at all. A pleasure to meet you both…Ah…Gobbos?" He tripped away and, as he went, they could hear him murmuring to himself: "What extraordinary people. And the father looking as young as the son. One never knows nowadays…"

20

The show was a great success, the first-night audience loving it. And Hennessy and Brooks went down a treat as the comic relief. Afterwards Brooks was so proud he appeared to have swelled up to twice his normal size.

The whole cast retired to Nixers, where Bad Bob had to shift pretty rapidly to keep up with the demands for service.

"Did you hear them laughing when I fell over?" Brooks enthused. "It was deadly..."

"But what about the music?" O'Brien put in. "Wasn't it a real razzle-dazzle? It was fandabadosia," he answered himself. "Yabadabadoo..."

He jumped in the air and on the way down met Swift going up. They slapped hands.

The noise grew as more and more people pushed their way in. When Hennessy saw Mercedes McGurk coming in, he set off to intercept her. She laughed that crinkle-eyed smile of hers when she saw him approaching but he was waylaid before he could get to her.

"Why're you in such a hurry, head?" Liz Finn asked him, suddenly appearing and blocking his way. "Stay and share some space and jaw a little.

What'd you think of me tonight? Pretty snazzy, wot?"

"You were great," Hennessy lied. "Standing ovations every time you opened your mouth…"

"You think there's a career in it for me?" the girl went on, ignoring his attempts to push past her. She had an elbow like a lance and it was doing its best to push its way through to his backbone.

"On the stage, you mean?"

"Maybe in films," the girl said dreamily. "If Madonna can do it, why can't I?"

"Do it? Do what?"

"Become a nun… What d'you think?" Furiously the girl punched him in the chest. "Freaking great, that's what I was. You think that band'd like me to front them. You know, the 4-Ups…"

That's an idea, Hennessy thought, then said it out loud.

"They're your friends, aren't they?" the girl cried. "You could mention it to them. You know, bend their ears…"

Hennessy scratched his head.

"Maybe if you talked to Swiftie…"

"Swift? The one with the pimples? The most chat I've ever had with him was to tell him to go spit in his fist once when he asked me for a date."

"Swift asked you for a date?"

"Yeah… Don't they all?"

"Well, the sly old dipstick…"

Liz looked at him under her eyebrows, a come-on that as usual he failed to recognise.

"So, what about the barbecue, then?" she asked him. "You know it's planned for the last night of the show..."

"Down on Dollymount Strand, I believe."

"Well?"

"Well what?"

"For cryin' out loud!" The girl looked at the heavens as though for sympathy. "Aren't you going to ask me?"

"Ask you to come with me? To the barbecue?"

"No, to the knees-up over in Buckingham Palace. You're some looper, you are."

"What about Maxie Bacon?"

"What about him?"

"Yeah," Hennessy said, thinking fast, "what about him..?"

A plan had suddenly begun to form in his head, a way to get even with Mad Max for all the hassle he'd caused him. Suddenly he was in even more of a hurry to get away from Liz Finn. As a matter of fact it was imperative that he get away from everyone and be by himself so that he could work out the details of this beautiful firework-burst of inspiration that had exploded in his brain-box.

"Sure, I'll take you," he told the girl, "but I'll meet you down there. We'll have a ball," he promised, but already he was moving away, forgetting about Mercedes McGurk, about Brooks, about Swift, about everything. Only Mad Max Bacon hovered in his mind's eye, and he was getting smaller by the minute.

21

Rock Around Shylock drew full, loud, enthusiastic and appreciative houses for every one of its four nights. Parents as well as pupils entered into the spirit of the thing, and the general consensus was that the school had a success on its hands.

The two highlights of each evening were Hennessy and Brooks as the Gobbo father and son and the disco dancing of Ben and Ella, two students from St Jude's who had almost reached professional status and intended making that particular form of activity their life's work.

After the speeches and presentations and mutual back-slapping on the Sunday night, Hennessy came out to the front of the hall to where his grandparents were waiting for him. Molly demonstrated by sign language that they were both deaf from the volume of sound but she was able to convey that they had liked the show.

"Brooksie and myself'll just come up home with you," Hennessy mouthed at her. "Just to make sure you get there safely..."

Ignoring their protests he shepherded them out and the four of them climbed into the Volkswagen. Because of her temporary deafness, Molly drove more carefully than usual and, except for an unfortunate fat man with a limp who decided to cross the road on an amber light, she left everyone she passed with a reasonable amount of peace of mind.

When they reached the driveway in front of the house, Hennessy said that he'd put the car into the garage for her. Molly passed over the keys and herself and Pop went inside. When he was sure that they were safely out of sight he got out, leaving the engine idling. He went into the garage. In a moment he was back out carrying a large coil of steel-strengthened rope over one arm.

Brooks helped him to put this in the boot and they both piled back into the front seats.

"Are you sure you're able to drive this thing?" Brooks asked anxiously. "How many miles have you logged up?"

"Well, I've driven tractors in Africa. And my father's Peugeot 405..."

"On the main road?"

"Not quite on the main road, no. But what difference does it make? I know how to change gear, I know how to brake, I know how to stop. What else is there?"

Brooks looked dubious but he held his tongue.

To demonstrate his prowess Hennessy took his foot off the clutch. The car being in fourth gear, it lurched forward and stalled.

"Oops, sorry..."

He switched on the engine again, rammed the

gear lever into first, took his foot off the clutch and the car leaped forward like a greyhound coming out of the trap. Luckily there was no traffic on the main road; otherwise there would have been a spectacular confrontation.

He was halfway down the North Circular and wondering why the car was making so much noise when he realised that as well as having it in first gear, he'd also left the handbrake on. He changed to third, hugged the left-hand kerb, took one hand off the wheel and told a petrified Brooks: "There, I told you I could drive!"

They made the coast road without mishap and turned towards Clontarf. It was fully dark now, but the sky, a luminous bluey grey, still retained some light. It was a warm, calm night, ideal for a barbecue.

When they came to the turn-off for the wooden bridge that led out on to Dollymount Strand, Swift and O'Brien detached themselves from the shadows and flagged down the car.

Hennessy rolled down the window.

"Any sign of him yet?"

"Not unless he can walk on water."

"Don't worry, he'll come. He knows that I'm supposed to be meeting Liz Finn at the barbecue..."

"How does he know?"

"I wrote and told him. Signed the letter 'a friend'."

"What makes you thing he can read?"

"Well if he can't he can surely get someone to read it for him."

Swift shook his head.

"Everyone else's been here hours ago," he said. "There'll be nothing left to eat or drink."

"Okay. Get in…"

They climbed in and Hennessy gingerly nosed the car out on to the narrow bridge. The sun-dried boards groaned and buckled under the wheels, causing Brooks to bless himself.

When they got to the end of the bridge, they could see the flare of the bonfire where the other members of the cast were disporting themselves. The sounds of laughter and singing came to them through the stillness of the night.

Hennessy drove the car down to the hard-packed sand, turned it in a wide sweep and set it facing back the way they had come. He turned the ignition off, the engine gave a few happy clanks and bangs, then gratefully died. The first part of the plan had been accomplished: now it only needed Mad Max to turn up on cue and the rest could be put into operation.

The festivities were going strong when they strolled up. They were greeted by catcalls and jeers and asked if the pubs had closed at last. Most of the food consisted of take-aways but a few hardy souls were doing their best to roast sausages in the fire, an undertaking that resulted merely in burnt offerings and scorched fingers.

In the flickering firelight it was difficult to distinguish faces. Hennessy wandered about; then saw Liz Finn and halted in his tracks. To his surprise she seemed to be involved in a wrestling match with

Ben, of the Ben and Ella dance team, while the same Ella looked on, glowering. This didn't put him out, however, for it kept her out of his way. His attention had shifted elsewhere...

And that elsewhere, namely Mercedes McGurk, was sitting with a group of her friends nearby. When she saw him hovering, she made room for him and he flopped down gratefully in the warm sand, accepting a chip from a greasy parcel that was offered to him.

Ever since the business of his locking Mercedes in the room and his letting her out again and the manner in which she'd accepted it, he had seen Liz Finn fade from his daydreams and Mercedes appear front and centre. She might not have Liz's colourful turn of phrase or her hardness but she possessed a good sense of humour, a sunny personality and she was smaller in height than he was. There'd be no looking up to *her*.

As though sensing his regard, the girl turned and looked at him and gave him her crinkly-eyed smile. His heart did a flip-flop. He was wondering if he dared put his arm around her when he suddenly noticed that she was in fact gazing out over his head and that the grin that he had thought destined for him was really meant for someone else.

A boy of about eighteen had come into the circle of firelight, a tall muscular-looking guy with a toothy grin and a mop of blond hair. "Tom...," Mercedes breathed, her eyes aglow, her expression undeniably welcoming.

"Tom?" Hennessy asked. "Tom who?"

The guy with the teeth and hair took her hands and she pulled him down beside her, effectively dislodging Hennessy in the process. He was pushed out onto a patch of cold sand which the heat from the fire hadn't reached.

Mercedes and the new arrival went into a clinch and, when she had eventually to come up for air, the girl beheld a pair of eyes glaring accusingly at her.

"Oh, I forgot," she said, her tone a mixture of sugar and spice but not all things nice, "you haven't met Tom, have you? This is my boyfriend, Tom Brown."

"Your what?" Hennessy inquired.

"My boyfriend. Tom's just finished his first year in university. He's going to be a dentist."

"You never told me you had a boyfriend."

"You have trouble with that, chum?" Tom said, addressing Hennessy for the first time.

"Only when I suck it. When I chew on it, it's okay."—Hennessy wondered what it would be like to pull out Tom's flashing white teeth one by one, preferably without the benefit of either gas or an anaesthetic. For that matter, a hammer and chisel would do the job very nicely.

But Tom wasn't in the mood for trading insults: "Why don't you push off?" he said belligerently. "Go on, take a powder. Scram. Get lost..."

"You mean, you want me to go?"

Tom flashed those too bright teeth of his again.

"That's it, now you've got it. That wasn't too

difficult for your tiny mind, was it?"

Hennessy stood up, brushed the sand from his trousers with as much dignity as he could muster and moved out of the circle of firelight. He had only gone a few paces when he started running, his arms windmilling, his feet digging into the beach. His course was erratic: one minute he was splashing along in the surf, the next he was up and into the sand dunes. He fell, got up again, shouted into the streaming air. When he came to a hard-packed stretch he did a forward somersault, then a back flip. He stood on his hands, walked a little way upside down, overbalanced, toppled.

Immediately he was up and running again, the wind in his face. He kept going until he could run no more. He felt utterly spent, yet at the same time exhilarated. At that moment he needed no one, no thing, nothing. He was part of the air, at one with the sand, the beach, the water. The thought came to him that maybe if he tried, closed his eyes and wished with all his heart, he could fly. To lift off in a slow banking curve, wheel in over the bonfire, then move high into the night sky over Dublin, so high that the lights would be only pinpricks in the darkness and sound would be the silence of no sound at all.

"Where've you been, then?"

Brooks looked questioningly at his friend, Hennessy, noting his ruffled appearance and wet trouser legs.

"I went for a run."

"A run?"

"Have you never done that? When you just wanted to get away from everything? To tear along until the only thing that matters to you is when you're going to stop..."

"Naw," Brooks said, looking sorrowful. "Whenever I'm worried about anything, I eat sweets. That's why I'm so fat."

"You must worry a lot then..."

Hennessy sat down wearily. O'Brien was strumming his guitar, Swift beating out the time with two large stones. The assembled company—at least those who hadn't sloped off into the dunes—was singing a sad song, and it appeared as if the party was dying of its own lack of energy. Even the fire was collapsing in on itself, throwing up showers of sparks that whirled like fire-flies in the night-time darkness.

Hennessy was idly dribbling sand through his fingers and thinking gloomily how you could never trust girls, when suddenly there was a great stuttering roar that shattered the peace and quiet of the scene. Looking quickly to his left he saw a dark shape moving with a rushing burst of energy, a shape that he was more than familiar with, the leather-clad Mad Max Bacon astride his iron horse and galloping up at a rate of knots.

He barely had time to scramble aside before the ultimate warrior arrived, the sand furrowing on either side of him like the Red Sea opening. Just as he came to the fire, he caused the bike to rear up and he went through the blazing embers on his back wheel, scattering them in all directions.

The remains of the fire wasn't the only thing he scattered. The revellers took off too, no one waiting to see how anyone else was, but each fearful for his or her safety and anxious to be away.

"Hold it," Hennessy roared, when he saw Brooks, Swift and O'Brien on their feet and poised for flight. Having to shout above the din, he told them: "You know what the plan is. Brooks, you come with me, and you two get to your posts."

They had to be fast on their feet, for Bacon was already on his return journey and anything in his path was liable to be turned into mush.

Once again Hennessy was running in that old zig-zag pattern, thinking feverishly that it was getting to be a habit. To take the heat off Brooks, who was labouring along in his wake, he suddenly stopped, waited till Bacon was almost on him, then stepped aside bullfighter fashion to let his enraged enemy slew past him.

He had to do this a couple more times before he got to the car, but the soft going helped him, the heavy bike proving difficult for Bacon to handle as the sand gave way beneath the wheels.

When he finally arrived he wrenched open the door and dived in. He had left the keys in the ignition and, with a fervent prayer to the God of motor car starters, he switched on the engine. His prayer was answered, for it immediately came to life, surging into a healthy roar as his foot pressed on the accelerator.

The passenger door thudded open and Brooks fell in, a sound like a death-rattle issuing from his tortured throat.

"For someone who can't run," Hennessy had time to say, "you didn't do too badly there."

He put the car into motion, and not a moment too soon. The front wheel of the pursuing motor bike slammed into the rear bumper, causing the ancient Volkswagen to leap forward and making its occupants risk whiplash.

Hoping that Swift and O'Brien were safely in place, Hennessy steered for the gap that gave access from the beach to the cement strip of road that led to the bridge. He pressed his foot to the floor and the car skidded across the sand, rubber whining and every bolt and screw shuddering.

In his haste he had forgotten to put on the lights but the silver sheen of moonlight illuminated surfaces and threw edges into sharp focus. A huge spray of sand fountained up behind the car, causing Bacon to slow down in order to get his bearings. This suited Hennessy's plan because it enabled him to put some distance between himself and his pursuer.

They thundered up to the exit and through it, then Hennessy had to wrench hard at the wheel to prevent the car from going straight on into the sea. He made the strip of road with centimetres to spare, slowed down and brought the Volkswagen to a halt.

"Come on," he commanded a stunned Brooks, then, flinging the door open, he stumbled out.

He was just in time to see Bacon speed up the

slight incline from the beach, the beam of his headlamp cutting a swathe through the darkness. Dimly he could discern the figures of Swift and O'Brien, as they bent and pulled at the steel rope which they had left loosely looped around the cement bollards that marked the entrance to the beach. They both leaned back to take the strain, and the rope twanged as it became taut.

As Bacon came up to it, it took him under the arms and, with a suddenness that even the watchers found bone-jarring, jerked him backwards, still in a sitting position. He disappeared into the night but his steed continued on, up and over the road and then in a perfect and glorious arc out over the sea. The breeze of its passing ruffled Hennessy's hair and it seemed like an eternity before there came a thunderous splash and, a little later, a glug-glug-glugging sound like a hungry giant gratefully swallowing the last of his dinner.

"So passes the glory of the world," Hennessy muttered gleefully, turning eagerly to Brooks.

"Great balls of fire," Brooks breathed almost prayerfully. Then he too gave vent to his feelings by powerfully breaking wind.

"Was I right or was I right?" Hennessy crowed, as the four of them capered about, slapping hands and whooping like Red Indians. "I told you my plan would work. Brains will always win out over brawn..."

They war danced about a bit more, then Brooks suddenly sobered them up when he said: "What if we've killed him? He could've broke his neck..."

They stopped and thought about it.

"I suppose we'd better go and look for him," Hennessy finally said. "That is if he hasn't been catapulted over Howth Head."

They went searching for their fallen foe and it was the sound of muffled groans that eventually led them to where he was sprawled. He was lying on his back in the sand, his arms and legs thrown wide as though he was nailed there. The groans were issuing from the fishbowl helmet that he still had on his head.

"Well, at least he's not dead," a relieved Brooks redundantly informed them.

Hennessy marched up to the inert form, put his foot on his chest and gave a Tarzan ape call. The sound echoed weirdly among the dunes and a number of heads appeared to see what the matter was.

Swift bent and removed the helmet, and Bacon's puffed and purple features were revealed. His eyes were open and his tongue drooped out of the corner of his mouth.

"I suppose someone should give him the kiss of life," Swift suggested.

They stood and looked down at him, but no one volunteered to perform the service.

Suddenly Hennessy bent closer, staring intently. He pursed his lips and whistled softly. Then he said in an awe-struck tone, "Well I'll be a monkey's uncle... Will you just look at that!"

The other three crowded round to see what Hennessy had seen. Then they too gave exclamations of surprise.

Probably because of the force of his impact with the rope, Mad Max's eyes were no longer crossed. Instead the pupils had returned to a normal position, and his gaze, unblinking and vertical, was sending its beam straight and true at the stars twinkling in the night sky above him.

22

It was the end of May. The exams were looming—so was the World Cup! For the moment, though, the sun was shining, flowers were in bloom, God was in his heaven and all was right with the world.

Hennessy, Brooks, Swift and O'Brien, the Four Just Men, were sitting at a table outside Nixers discussing their plans for the summer. Hennessy was due to spend part of it in Africa but he would not be going until August. Brooks was in the process of telling them that his mother had signed him up for a course in the West of Ireland to enable him to improve his Irish.

"That's funny," Swift commented. "O'Brien and myself have been offered a month's engagement playing Irish music in a pub in a place called Tóin le Gaoith. Lawless, of all people, put us in the way of it. Said it was time we did something for our country…"

"Do you know any Irish music?"

"Not really. But it shouldn't be too difficult to learn. It's all a bit yowdeldy-dowdeldy, isn't it?"

The thought of two heavy-rock merchants like Swift and O'Brien playing Irish jigs and reels caused Hennessy to snort with laughter.

"You'll probably have to wear leprechaun outfits,"

he told them. "And it'd be just as well if you toned down your Dublin accents. They don't take kindly to strangers in them thar neck o' the woods…"

"Well, it's good money," O'Brien said defensively. "And now that my old dear's told me I've to go back to Jude's for another year, maybe it'd be as well if I pick up on the old Gaelic…"

"You're going back?" Hennessy said delightedly.

"Yeah…and so is Swifty. He's under orders as well."

"You're not?"

Hennessy grinned at Swift, who was trying to look mad.

"I was given two choices," he admitted. "If I want to keep up the music, go back and do the Leaving Cert and have something to fall back on. Otherwise get a job. And"—he shrugged—"as jobs are scarce, what could I do?"

"That's great," Hennessy enthused. "It means we'll be together again next year. We'll have mighty crack."

"That is, if Maxie Bacon doesn't get us first," Brooks reminded them gloomily.

"Are you joking?" Hennessy gave him a friendly punch on the shoulder. "Mad Max is a thing of the past. He's so delighted at seeing straight again that his whole personality's changed. He goes about now smiling and nodding at everyone, doing good works, lighting candles in churches, helping old ladies across streets. It's like St Paul's conversion on the road to Damascus. Old Maxie's been touched by the Lord and is the better man for it..."

After the night of the barbecue they had all gone about in fear and trepidation, but the wrath of the Evil One had not descended on their heads. That day at low tide Bacon's motorbike had surfaced out of the slime of Dublin Bay like King Arthur's fabled sword Excalibur. However, no one had come to salvage it, and now it was a landmark every time the tide went out.

Of Mad Max himself, nothing had been seen. He had not come back to school, and Liz Finn had also taken herself off to work full-time at her hairdressing job.

The last few weeks of the term had been uneventful after the fun and frolics that had preceded them. The only event of note was that Mr House had set fire to his office one Friday afternoon—it was generally felt that it was the friction caused by his rate of exit that had ignited the spark—and the fire brigade had to be called to extinguish it.

"You know," Brooks said, pausing in his efforts to demolish a small mountain of ice cream, "that place you mentioned, Tóin le Gaoith, is close to where I'm going in Connemara. Wouldn't it be great if Henno were to do the course too, and then the gang wouldn't be split up at all?"

"That's a thought."

Hennessy squinted into the afternoon sunshine. Who knew what kind of fun they could have if they all went West together?

That very evening he broached the subject to his grandparents. They were sitting out on the flagstones behind the house enjoying the evening warmth, Pop half asleep, Molly painting yet another giant sign and from time to time complaining about the state of the garden to her unresponsive menfolk. Mabel was perched in a tree nearby, one wing outstretched and her beak busily searching under it for signs of animal life.

"An Irish course in Connemara?" Molly paused in her exertions and gazed suspiciously at her grandson. "What're you up to now?"

Putting on his innocent face, Hennessy assured her that perfecting his Irish was the only thing on his mind: "It's the tradition coming out in me, you see. The culture, the sense of history...Fionn and the Fianna...Cú Chulainn...Peig Sayers...Brendan Behan..."

"Did they all come from Connemara?"

"Well, I'm sure some of them did."

Hennessy caught Pop's disbelieving eye and looked quickly away.

"Well, whatever you're up to, it's not such a bad idea," Molly said thoughtfully.

"That's it," Hennessy encouraged her. "And I happen to know that there's places left. Mr Lawless is organising it. All you have to do is ring him..."

Pop and Molly looked at one another, then Pop shrugged and said, "Might as well let him go. He'll pester us until you do..."

"Pester us until you do," Mabel suddenly

squawked, just to show that she'd been listening.

But Hennessy had his hands behind his head and was leaning blissfully back to gaze into the evening sun. Like the optimist with his pint of stout, he was thinking of the half of the year that was left rather than the half that was already gone. And the thought of Liz Finn or Mercedes McGurk hardly entered his mind...

Children's
POOLBEG

To get regular
information about
our books and authors join

THE POOLBEG
BOOK CLUB

To become a member of
THE POOLBEG BOOK CLUB
Write to Anne O'Reilly,
The Poolbeg Book Club,
Knocksedan House,
Swords, Co. Dublin.
Please write clearly and make sure to include
all the following details: Name, full address,
date of birth, school.